100 Days
of
Happiness

KRISTY BERRIDGE

*B*orn in Perth, Western Australia in 1982, Kristy Berridge was ushered into the world in a decade of bad hair, parachute pants, and blue eye shadow. Fortunately, she managed to  avoid all three by immersing herself in the business of growing up and hitched a ride with her fun-loving and adventure-filled parents to the sunny state of Queensland. Here she completed most of her education.

Besides learning that boys *don't* have cooties, and that algebra *wouldn't* kill her, she pointedly set the path of her high school career towards success in Art and English-based subjects, and won numerous awards for her efforts.

After high school she went on to study Graphic Design and Illustration at James Cook University, furthered her studies at the local TAFE college with an Interior Design course, and then undertook a three-year Design course at Rhodec International in London.

Clearly the girl just can't sit still. Kristy now pens fanciful fiction novels in her spare time finding creative new ways to scare herself and others in the dead of night, promote girl-power with gritty action sequences and of course, highlight teenage idiosyncrasies with hard-hitting hormonal moments of lust.

She currently resides in Cairns, procrastinates constantly, now studies nutrition and tries desperately to avoid the delicious temptation that is the peanut butter aisle at the supermarket.

Shadow Ink Press
P.O Box 352n, Cairns North, Queensland 4870 Australia
Email: shadowinkpress@hotmail.com

First published in Australia 2016 - This edition published 2016
Copyright © Kristy Berridge 2016
Cover design, typesetting: Shadow Ink Press
The right of Kristy Berridge to be identified as the Author of the Work has been asserted in accordance with the Copyright, Designs and Patents Act 1988.

Berridge, Kristy
100 Days of Happiness
ISBN: 9780987524782

Acknowledgements

I would like to thank everyone who played a part in this one hundred day journey. Although no names were ever mentioned—and the book is mostly a work of fiction—you know who each of you are and I thank you for your honesty, jovial nature, trust and above all … endless support in this comedic exposure.

A small, but no means menial message to my ever wonderful publishing company Shadow Ink Press for all the time and effort it took in realising this novel into actuality.

Day One

April fool's day—a feast for the prankster and a trap for the gullible. I wasn't entirely sure which category I resided—perhaps I was a fool regardless, a fool destined to be punished by my own lack of self-awareness and general absence of life's ambition.

Surely I was a fool for believing I could redeem the last thirty years of lack-lustre tidings and carve a new existence; one filled with adventure, beauty, true honest-to-God love; the kind of magnificence I might one day reflect upon with genuine fondness and awe.

Was it a pipe dream, a childish wish to hope to inspire what most took for granted: Love? Creativity? Wealth?

This journey was not solely for the betterment of oneself, but for inspired happiness in the people around me I cherish. I'd questioned the possibility of finding happiness over one hundred days when the pessimist within knew that seventy-three were based around the monotony of the working week.

Dilemma.

Work … a necessary evil; an absolute certainty oiling the wheels of each daily grind. Unassisted by regular coffee shots and the bloody machine (me), would rust, seize and re-educate those present with words rhyming with 'truck' and 'punt'.

Don't get me wrong; I'd always been rather fond of my job, but some days, high-fiving people in the face with a chair shouldn't be a fantasy.

I believed that within the restrictive walls of my nine-to-five environment, I'd find the greatest challenge—not fending off lawsuits from disgruntled people with chair kindling lodged in facial orifices—searching for peace while inspiring a network of happy bystanders to quiet the aching disappointment I often felt after giving up a thriving career as a professional stripper.

Kidding!

Questioning myself regarding my lack of useful qualifications in pursuit of happiness occurred regularly. Should I have stayed in college? Should I have gone to clown school and joined the circus? Should I have married a ninety-year-old millionaire for security and his marketable stash of Viagra?

Who knew? Perhaps if the answer had been 'yes' I would've rocked a red nose or killed the old geezer with this crazy thing I can do with my tongue. I'd have inherited millions, but I'd also never know. I couldn't edit the past or myself. The trick was to accept the present; cherish it for what it was; the life I'd made.

This was where I mostly came unstuck and tumbled down the rabbit hole. The inner dialogue of insecurity bred in this place of uncertainty. That was why I'd decided to seek something brushed with simplicity—one hundred happy days to reconcile the past, accept the present and plan for a future worthy of silver-screen adaptation. Well—at the very least if I employed realism—dreams realised into proud achievements.

Today—classified as the fool's occasion on the calendar—also marked the initiation of this ambitious project; create one hundred days plucked from moments of heightened emotion, life-altering events and the tom-foolery I often invested in.

My audience?

It had been and will be, any poor bastard who reads this mostly true, regularly embellished account of my deluge into adult diary writing. Social networking sites would become a tool in which this embarrassing self-exposure would be unveiled. The reader would never witness these accounts of daily drivel otherwise.

So what was the purpose of this idea? Was it to give Hallmark ideas for future carded declarations of love and whimsy?

No.

I hoped to inspire people to step outside the box, be brazen with life choices, dispel tears and self-doubt where possible and hopefully, I'd encourage smile propagation in others.

Realistically, no one could be happy, rational and calm every minute of the day. Hell, I'd been known to chuck a tantrum if someone didn't refill the kettle or if I was asked too many stupid questions in a row. The point of the experiment was to try.

I confess: I was not clever enough to realise this idea on my own. Do-gooders had spammed my social media feed with the concept—responsible for the spread of both good and bad social experimentation. In this instance, I was enthusiastic to embrace the philosophy of promoting positivity. Unlike the 'free hugs' agenda that had spread globally several months ago inspiring rash investment in vats of hand sanitiser, being happy meant investing in more self-development time and those around me.

This social experiment was exactly what I needed after months of tumultuous activity (soon to be expanded upon in greater, glorious detail). To spend time warmed by riotous belly laughs—or to ache from an overly-stretched smile—was an improvement on self-inflicted divorce proceedings.

Admittedly, my usual perky-self had unnecessarily buried her head in a lot of sandy bullshit. Positivity had taken a nose-dive as past events and expectations for the future poured icy cynicism over my exposed soul. What had once been so simple inside my head had now become laced with hidden agenda—part of me searching weird sources of drama I clearly lacked in a previous life.

My insecurities?

Multiple.

I'd always struggled to trust my instincts, believe in myself and embrace my intelligence. If definitions had been clear-cut, I'd be classified a social spastic, constantly searching for something— anything to help the true me emerge.

But I digress …

So, back to April Fool's day; back to my errand to etch happiness in my life and the lives of others; a task so daunting I almost reneged.

Almost …

Most days you'll find me glued to a vinyl swivel chair, answering phones and serving the public. My smile: genuine, but was often a well-tailored mask I slipped into comfortably. Six years of unending change had created a working-class shell—a woman outstanding in her job description, but going through the motions for the sake of a decent pay-check.

It was time for a change.

So what happened on this day, the first of one hundred laden with mounting expectation?

Nothing.

Today was ordinary, a day just like any other. The sky had not rained cats and dogs, pigs hadn't flown and men hadn't unanimously started putting the toilet seat down. But, I'd chosen to see more, feel more and listen more. Numerous mental snapshots of laugh-out-loud moments and precious minutes such as *The Boss* avoiding lapsing into a boredom coma reigned supreme.

I'd felt compassion for a woman with triplets; three rambunctious boys who'd run her ragged; their little legs powering them around the waiting room as she'd given chase. Compassion quickly shifted to idle thoughts of tying their shoelaces together, slapping them over the back of the head and yelling: 'Sit down, you little bastards or I'll knock you out!'.

The Boss was most grateful I'd kept that opinion to myself.

I'd then laughed mercilessly at a customer presenting with 'Cockburn' as a surname. Mindful of the amusement factor, I'd run around the office telling everyone there was a penile emergency in the waiting room. To then have asked the poor guy to repeat his name twice and then spell it out was merely for added, personal entertainment.

I was going to hell.

Next, though not as lively as 'Mr Burnt Dick' and 'Mrs Needs Contraception', I'd quickly become awed, inspired and jealous of a texting war that had occurred between my parents. *The Mother* had messaged me about their sonnets of love and all things sickeningly sweet. After twenty-six years of marriage, I'd been warmed to know that my parents still gazed upon one another as if the world began and ended in their combined embrace.

Maybe there was something to learn from this seemingly endless union. I couldn't apply it to my past, but the future was yet to be written. Finding happiness in the pleasure of another's company; exploring the possibility of magnetic touch; to feel the unending desire and devotion from another, equally compelled to seek it with me? Now *that* was something to look forward to.

One step at a time.

Today I looked forward to clocking off, showing work the big middle finger and careening from the car-park as fast as my two-litre engine could burn rubber. A recent brush with the law should've lightened my lead foot. I had no low-cut singlet to save me should a ticket have ensued and yet, I pursued unhealthy speeds in the name of post-work relaxation.

Tonight a lone cop fingered his walkie-talkie on a side street—probably sipping cold coffee as he waited for something exciting to happen in my quiet, little suburb. I hadn't been exciting enough. I was ignored, barely glanced at as I sped past. Maybe it had been 'Dunkin' Donut time' and he'd had his lips smacked around too much sugary crust to notice.

Lucky me.

When I arrived home, rustling through the letter box unearthed junk-mail and a letter from my bank containing two, one hundred dollar gift cards for a major department store. What the fuck? When did a bank ever reward its investors with anything other than monthly fees and interest?

I planned to spend the vouchers as soon as possible before they realised they'd made a terrible mistake.

So, all-in-all, day one had a few highlights. Happiness had been found in trivial pursuits, laughs had been in decent supply and luck seemed to have been on my side. With ninety-nine days to go, I chose to try and remain positive, search for the humour in every situation and pray that my pessimism didn't ultimately win the day.

Day Two

*T*oday was my birthday; Father Time had made it his life's mission to etch wrinkles on every patch of smooth skin remaining. Despite the euphoric rush of birthday celebrations, turning thirty-two was a candle blow-out away from looking like a ruddy-fleshed geriatric claiming ownership of a colostomy bag. I already peed every hour, had more lines on my face than a bloody atlas and cringed at my cracking knee caps.

I shouldn't act disappointed by the inevitable advancement of my age. I should seek positivity from this cornerstone and acknowledge that age brought wisdom and experience. But how could happiness be found in knowing I'd soon have a worse bladder and a face that could potentially age to look like old biker boots?

I tried to take note of the key word in that admission … 'potentially'.

Thankfully, my declining age hadn't been keeping pace with 'The Crypt Keeper'. Call me a hypochondriac, but these were the issues that often consumed my thoughts. This girl had some insecurities—probably still did.

Did I mention I was also the artistic type—creative to the core? No?

That might seem obvious given my overly voluptuous, descriptive nature. A little embellishment here and there was entirely necessary in creating good fiction. Going to the grocery store would not be the same without a crazy shoot-out or local gang-bang by the ice-cream fridge. Hence, I'd try to keep it interesting … I hope.

Right, back on point.

It was my birthday today and I'd made plans of an extraordinarily stupid nature. The idea had been to prove my self-worth, deny my thirty-two years of age and go on a physically challenging hike where I traversed the biggest mountain in my region fondly known as 'Satan's Asshole'.

'Satan's Asshole' was sure to tone my sagging behind and sweat off the previous night's indulgence (muffins), but all plans I'd had to climb and conquer were quickly put on hold. *The Mother* had lectured me about rapists with bushy beards; *The Bestie* assaulting me with concepts of creepers with guns. From what it sounded like, I needed to be on the lookout for Ned Kelly.

I considered ignoring what had been the good advice of those that cared about me most. If I also ignored my defiance for just a moment, it would've been possible to see that these kill-joys were onto something. Harsh reality dictated that I would most probably break my legs, get lost in the wilderness or run out of water and food. I'd probably be violated by a bush pig while I was at it.

Okay, point made.

Exercise was not on the agenda today; a block run, a beach walk or even a little hike up the point was rebuked by God himself. The heavens opened and a freak rainstorm challenged any outdoor activities.

My rebuttal was a swift north-facing arm raise followed by a one-finger salute. I hoped the ensuing thunderstorms of biblical proportions weren't a direct result of the flip-off.

I sulked and pouted for some time, mostly aimed at the open refrigerator door and its lack of contents. I had no idea why I was always hungry or who kept eating all my chocolate during these desperate times of inside-bound activity.

I bummed around social media for a while, responding in kind to the growing number of posts that wished me well despite my rainy fucking birthday. I cheered up marginally when my new friend—*The Cockney*—sent a personal message. We'd been chatting online for a while now; his rather innocent approach to conversation had me curious.

We'd never met in person yet, whenever we talked, it felt as if we'd known each other for years. So easy was our interaction, that as we discussed food, travel or any of life's nuances, time slipped by, reality would catch up and then neither would concur that conversing in person might actually be eventful.

I'd considered the possibility that we might stay in our virtual world of instant messaging for the foreseeable future. After all, *The Cockney* was smart, witty and completely endearing; I was, well … me. How we'd interact if we ever physically met was the greatest mystery of all. He was this idealistic character; perfect in my mind; destined to be kept at arm's length for the sake of my backwards approach to my ideal match. I didn't want to think about how inadequate I felt when comparing myself to someone I believed could very well be …

Right; random speculation aside and birthday wishes responded to, I decided to change my moody attitude. I could continue to sit idle with my thumb up my butt or spend an obscene amount of money—a fate worse than death for my long-suffering bank account.

Truth?

I dropped five hundred dollars in less than an hour.

I'd like to say before blowing my savings I'd found my latent humanity and donated the funds to save orphan dogs or feed refugees in Somalia, but it would have been bullshit. Lace, elastin and G-strings had taken my fancy. I'd wandered into a lingerie store and hadn't emerged until the wicked urge to be swathed in silky undergarments maxed my credit card.

At least the purchases aided in the fight against gravity.

Did I mention the make-up and several needless outfits that also made it into the shopping bags? No? Then forget I said anything. Cancer sucks and bus fares should be free for pensioners.

An extravagant day of frivolous expenditure aside, my mood had improved. I wouldn't have thought that my current course towards shopper's happiness could've been dulled; not even the depleted funds of my bank account could bring me down. What sent me plummeting into the depths of despair was a text from *The Current Squeeze* informing me that baseball practice was more important than my birthday dinner.

His logic was flawed and so was my ongoing interest in this twat—but since I failed to inform him how upset I was—I had no one to blame but myself. Why had I allowed this travesty to occur?

Insecurity.

We'd been dating a few months; the newness of such a relationship meant I remained awkward—uncertain how to act around someone who affected my libido and tampered with my common sense. I was confused by his emotional approach to our union and his ability to excite me in spite of our obvious differences. I was constantly torn between wanting to strike him with a tire iron and allowing him to bend me over the kitchen counter.

I headed home, certain I'd clock watch while taking my time to beautify for the after baseball, late-night date. Starvation was a very real possibility and fuelled my agitation. Several, very strong, milky coffees had helped fill the cavernous space within my stomach, but didn't dull the disappointment I felt.

Overanalysing the situation had also fuelled the agitation. I told myself that it was okay that *The Current Squeeze* had other plans coinciding with my preordained birthday celebrations. It was *okay* that he'd feed me somewhere close to midnight and it was *okay* that I'd fobbed off friends and family to spend the evening with *him*.

At this stage, I started fantasising about the tyre iron again.

By the time he arrived smelling like soap, leather and sex—dished out compliments like he was serving our entrée—my eager motor mouth lost all throttle. A deluge of reprimands were lodged within my trachea; I gushed over the armful of presents he shoved in my direction instead.

I hadn't received a birthday present in years—not because my parents were assholes or my ex-husband was inattentive—it was a result of adulthood. We neither expected nor required a gift to celebrate our declining age, nor did we desire what we could easily purchase for ourselves; so the ribboned box and accompanying card were a novelty.

Despite wanting to stay angry, I quickly forgave his misdemeanours and marvelled at the fact he'd absolutely nailed my taste—something most people never accomplish. The delicate silver chain enhanced my feelings. I'd been desperately trying to avoid that. Feelings were … complicated.

Adorned with expensive jewellery, *The Current Squeeze* finally realised my rumbling stomach was not the mating call of my weirdo neighbours. He promptly took me to a restaurant where the service was good and the food even better. We reminisced about our first few dates and mutual attraction. We held hands and kissed often. Everything seemed perfect; why wouldn't it be when our relationship was as fresh and shiny as the resplendent silver necklace he'd given me?

Doubt was a secret stalker, always looming and ever-present in my mind. So much was left unspoken and there was also much I didn't understand regarding dating, men and Playboy magazines. Being with him created both elation and confusion and I wasn't sure I liked how complicated it seemed to be. Shouldn't dating be wonderful?

I rapidly digressed to thoughts of dessert. The blissful distraction of sugar activated operation 'switch on second stomach'. Although I'd been gluttonous and decidedly unladylike during dinner, there was always room for chocolate.

I silently prayed that *The Current Squeeze* felt similarly about sharing dessert.

It was never an option.

Ever!

I plotted to throat-punch him if he convinced the waiter we'd carve up a meringue together. Silent plea heard—maybe distracted by the exuberant troop of singing waiters—he never had the opportunity. Free desserts were tossed around like Frisbees; I soon became the happy recipient of a mini Pavlova complete with kiddie sparklers.

I holstered my mental fist and licked my lips, aware that sugary goodness was imminent. I reached for the silverware, fulfilment so close I could taste it, but then …

I spotted the second spoon; so had *The Current Squeeze* who promptly tucked in.

I would like to say that an ambulance had been called to the gory scene as I sat and contemplated what I'd look like in prison stripes, alas, violence never reared its head. I remained mild-mannered and annoyingly unvocal … again. The only time I spoke up was after dinner, back in my apartment, lying horizontal on my Egyptian cotton sheets!

The new lingerie was well received after much inspection; the stolen kisses from earlier were soon upgraded to heavy petting. We gave the neighbours a run for their money; I stopped stressing about sharing dessert. Despite my lack of confidence to address issues within our relationship—in that moment—I was happy in his embrace, lulled by multiple orgasms and the promise of more nights like this.

That was enough for now.

Day Three

*B*ack to work; back to the daily grind; back to sighing audibly every few minutes and inaudibly every other moment in between. Phones rang off the hook and everyone had a fixed smile on their face. Mimicking turned into a trying little game that burned my cheeks.

I hadn't always been this negative about work. I used to belt out tunes across the front counter—despite my shocking vocal abilities—and regularly chatted with the elderly about dentures and haemorrhoids. Why? Smelly teeth and dangling ass decorations were especially interesting; however, at some point in my career, my enthusiasm had been shaken.

There'd been a hostage situation; I'd been absconded by a tall, dark and handsome stranger with a rippling six-pack and tawny-coloured skin. He'd forced me to touch his bulging biceps and kiss his thick, soft lips which had tortured all my pleasure hot spots. The final act had seen me hog-tied and violated with his tongue. I still wasn't certain if I'd ever recover from the situation.

Anyway, I suspected the negativity was a result of several ongoing and past factors.

I'd recently ended a fifteen year marriage. It had been a good marriage full of trust, warmth and mutual respect, but sadly had lacked passion and excitement. I'd loved my best friend and confidant, but in the end, women with my imagination and zest for life were never content with mediocre. We'd both deserved better.

Mediocre also explained how I felt about *The Current Squeeze* now. With the recent excitement of five, completely random and sexually exciting flings, I'd somehow let my past, present and possible future loves cloud my judgement, distract me from tasks at hand and confuse my feelings. How could I partition personal life from professional? How could I rediscover the joy I used to have offering kindness to others without wanting to slam their faces against a desk?

Hmm.

At least I'd been amused today even if I couldn't clarify it as happy. Belated birthday wishes flowed thick and fast and *The Boss* kept me on my toes with her Bi-Polar personality. She was on a mission to seek conversation with herself, muttering affirmations of: shit, stupid bitch, this is ridiculous and you've got to be fucking kidding me.

My favourite part was when she combined all expletives in a singular paragraph: 'Shit! This is ridiculous. Who touched my fucking keyboard? When I find the stupid bitch who ...' (Spills her coffee) 'You've got to be fucking kidding me.'

Paperwork and a mountain of deliveries saw me occupied until lunch. Time was filled with doe-eyed stares at the ridiculously handsome men who cluttered the waiting room or with trips to the toilet to increase my pedometer mileage.

Meanwhile, *The Boss* maintained her colourful profanities.

By midday my stomach waged war. Pitchforks held by the acidic fingers of the famished prodded my insides in savage desperation. I focused firmly on the belief that my tuna salad had been tossed lovingly by Neil Perry, despite droopy lettuce reflecting the lazy efforts of my early morning; 'I can't be fucked' mentality.

I made a concerted effort to avoid the café and bountiful treats offered up on display. I congratulated myself; I said no to sugar, eaten my tuna salad with a scowl and waited for *The Bestie* to join me so we could moan simultaneously. That was the best thing about work, sharing the tidings with someone with whom I adored, who made me laugh and believed emitting gas was another form of communication.

She had no issue derailing my ongoing diet and bought me a slab of Rocky Road to consume. I weighed the pros and cons of accepting the lavish treat, but soon devoured and conquered, licking my fingers clean, convinced my ass would soon have more fat friends to play with.

Since the slippery slope of calorie-laden consumption had already been mounted, my gluttonous indulgence continued with sushi, milky coffee and a hazelnut chocolate torte covered in whipped cream and gelato.

Diabetes and imaginary hostage situation aside, I made it my mission that day to invest in a happy moment. Planning seemed like a cheat's way to prosper, but drug addicts never questioned the origins of the next fix, merely the feeling supplied. I knew taking action and accomplishing my goals by way of advanced preparation would end in an expected result—one comparable to a drug addict—getting high.

Later that night, I got calorie wasted with *The Bestie* again. We talked a lot of shit and ate more junk food than I care to mention. We shifted boxes into her new house and disposed of the body of her ex-boyfriend she'd been keeping under the stairs. We both roared with laughter when his flaccid arm got caught in the car door and ripped from his body with gory ease. She wanted to throw it away, but the decorator within me showed her how useful it would be as a door stop.

It didn't matter that we regularly cleared up crime scenes or tossed sand at kids at the beach; I could relax with her and mostly avoided judgement because she appreciated me for the unique soul I'd become.

I wanted to remember and cherish these moments, expand upon them and also encourage them. It was these moments that would probably one day see me strapped to an electric chair, skin sizzling and brains fried.

But that was a problem for another day …

Day Four

*F*riday; it was safe to say that nothing bad had ever come from this day of the week. This celebrated ending led to wondrous beginnings; weekends potentially laden with yellow brick roads of bountiful happiness. The working week was left in the past and the future of the next two days brimmed with possibilities and exciting uncertainty.

The opportunity to head outdoors for adventure ranked highly. Spending time with friends and family—another way I optimized free time and avoided going bat-shit crazy. Drinking copious amounts of alcohol also helped, but to bypass a hangover and indulge the cute guy warming the mattress beside me—an even better option.

On this particular Friday—with its resemblance to OZ's wicked uncertainty—I avoided munchkins, tall tales of white witches and localised tornado warnings. It started like any other; an early morning bed-stretch followed by three minutes of digging crusty sleep from the corners of my over-tired eyes. When finally motivated to go vertical, I partook in what could only be described as a fabulous workout.

I chased resultant angina with mass murder, crushing helpless ants under nimble fingertips as they'd crawled across the kitchen with unnatural speed. Black blood spurted over chipped Laminex; I thought of protein, which led to thoughts of my poor diet. I needed to stop shovelling rubbish so I could exercise less!

I searched barren cupboards for signs of a healthy breakfast. I was determined after recent bingeing to eat more sugar-free cereal and watery porridge, but disaster struck. I was still cash-poor and had run out of milk, coffee and all other viable, healthy options. Thus I settled for gas-inducing avocado and eggs on colon-clogging white toast.

Anyway, I had to disregard thoughts of the upcoming weekend and my bloated belly. I still had eight hours of work to process and although clock hands moved faster than a two dollar hooker with your wallet, it was still tedious.

By five o'clock, everyone's lips blurred with irrelevant chatter. I'd had my fill of coffee, eaten somewhat healthy and may have even gone for a quick spin around the reception area on a wheelie chair for fun.

I'd been preoccupied for the majority of the day with thoughts of the evening to come. I wondered if *The Current Squeeze* might miss my absence that night or consider the separation unnecessary to speculate about. I suspected he'd given no thought at all to our temporary parting. This bothered me more than I realised.

As I headed to *The Bestie's* house, I tried clearing my mind. I gazed heavenward, taking in the burnt oranges and smudges of fuchsia that spliced the rapidly darkening sky; a beautiful distraction. So too had thoughts of the night's approaching agenda; a free concert; a vocal show from an old fart strumming a guitar.

The Bestie and I started the evening at our favourite bar, dressed to impress and ordering a plethora of cocktails that matched our mood; cock sucking cowboys and sex on the beach all round please!

Despite the alcoholic levity and our smokin' kit, she felt fat in her skinny jeans and t-shirt and I felt a set of nipple tassels would have better complimented my dress rather than studded heels. Perhaps self-conscious behaviour ran in the blood of all women, coursing through our veins with villainous intent. Perhaps we were all just idiots that should reassess our wardrobe before leaving the house.

A scrumptious dinner at a waterfront restaurant warmed our stomachs and provided ambience for continued conversation laced with sexual innuendo that led to a heated discussion regarding reasons why Highlanders wore kilts and played with swords.

'Cheque please!'

We didn't go anywhere. The heavens opened like they'd been sliced by a sloppy surgeon, spilling frigid rain in an effort to foil our escape. My hair quickly resembled an under-groomed poodle and *The Bestie* suddenly sported an afro.

'Another drink, please!'

Two hours after the concert's commencement, we stumbled through puddles and hedges, dodged tourists and played chicken with cars. We danced on park benches and finally made it to the venue; I shielded my thatch of frizzy hair with a ridiculously tiny purse and *The Bestie* bitched incessantly about her blistered toes.

The tunes pumped loudly and without rhythm. My geriatric bladder competed for attention and soon, bouncing from foot-to-foot could be classified a gangster dance move, a sure sign that the twenty minute queue for the bathroom would be my ultimate demise.

I focused back on the concert. The old fart was a no show thus far. I was two hours late and the gig was overrun by teenagers singing covers while a million sweaty bodies vied for a closer position by the stage.

By the time the old crooner clutched the microphone and belted his classic tunes, *The Bestie* had become a sweaty disaster and I was certain I was going to wet my pants.

I clutched my chest—not overcome with emotion—but fairly certain a heart attack loomed. The nearness of the stadium-sized speakers caused mass reverberation—like my vibrator in turbo mode—great for a moment but terrifying the next.

I'd like to say that I raged the night away, fisting the air with appreciation and ignoring the chest raping I received, but I didn't. I let the team down with my dodgy bladder and old-timer mentality.

We slunk through the crowd within half an hour, *The Bestie* shaking her head at my declining stamina and ringing ears. She'd re-tell this story for years to come. I already considered the shiny, blunt object I'd be slamming in her pie-hole.

Kidding.

It was a certainty that I'd be regularly ridiculed for my thirty minute attempt at concert attendance. I also had to invest in new underwear since there'd been insufficient public amenities.

At least I'd done something more than ordinary.

I'd shared a new experience with my best mate, got drunk, wet my pants (a little) and invested nothing but the cost of a few laughs. What had I received back?

A night full of memories, happiness and a wet patch to prove it!

Day Five

*I*t was finally the weekend, the very first Saturday and Sunday on what I fully expected to be an arduous one hundred day journey. I mostly pursued weekends with fervent enthusiasm and planned for as much adventure, fun—and if lucky enough—copious amounts of sex. Why? Because weekends were never complete without Monday morning regret or a mind blowing orgasm—preferably the latter.

I won't skip to the good parts without allowing the engaging tale to unfold. Nobody likes the bastard who ruins the plot of a good movie or blows the pun at the end of a well-told joke—then again—no one likes unnecessary build up without satisfactory release either.

Right. Perhaps it would be best clarified that adventure was indeed plentiful over the weekend despite lacklustre sexual tidings now known as: I didn't bloody get any or *The Current Squeeze* lost the directions to my vagina. Was I greedy?

Anyway, adventure! Admittedly, I didn't run the rim of a molten volcano or cage-dive with gluttonous Great White sharks, but I still made the most of my free time. Unfortunately, it wasn't spent pushing my pervy neighbour face-first down our apartment stairs or drowning his hormonal kids in the swimming pool. Today I morphed into Indiana Jones—minus the sweat-stained Akubra hat. I actually owned the whip, but that was a completely unrelated story in the making.

Sexual props and jungle-dreaming aside, Saturday morning was semi-wondrous. I slept an extra half hour and then begun the day with a workout that generated a level of perspiration saturation and body odour to epitomise true fitness dedication—a goal I'd often been ridiculed for.

I'd never kill myself to wear labelled lycra outfits or overdo crunches to journey forward to washboard abdominals. I celebrated exercise because of the fear factor—fear of getting fat again.

I used to be an Oompa Loompa. Fact. Ten years ago, I carried more rolls than a Swiss bakery and sported more chins than a Chinese phone book. I'd become terrified that a backward slide would find me writhing open-mouthed under a McDonald's soft-serve machine with six burgers balanced on my bulging belly. The simple truth was that I couldn't continue to look like Cindy Crawford if I ate small children while lounging on the sofa (I may or may not have fictionally elaborated my likeness to a supermodel).

Post workout, my thighs felt as though they'd copped a thorough beating and my pulse became alarmingly elevated. Punishing the asphalt now turned into running for my bedroom, praying that there was a flashing blue message from *The Current Squeeze*.

Nothing.

Nadda.

Zip.

Bitter disappointment clung to me like a blood-sucking parasite, digging doubt further into the nether regions of my mind. It was Saturday. Shouldn't he have wanted to see me? Shouldn't the weekend be filled with plans of our pending hook-up?

Dating was rapidly becoming a foreign concept I was certain I'd never master. Marriage I understood, but dating was like tripping on LSD; all fun and games until the high faded and the room spins endlessly.

How could I begin to understand men's thoughts and feelings, interpret their actions or translate hidden meaning in words with attached sentiment? Was there an instruction manual I could have downloaded from the internet outlining the dating do's and don'ts?

Would there be rules in this book? Would there be a million blank pages because they'd gotten bored and figured all women should be capable of reading minds? Would there be illustrations; an outline for the perfect blow job or the ramifications of leaving your toothbrush behind?

I needed to understand these foreign creatures and know when to let these strangers into my life. Should I lay myself bare and offer my soul for the taking in the name of emotional honesty? Or should I linger on the precipice of caution, ignore the desire to explore with hopefulness, passion and enthusiasm while I waited to exhale? I'd probably die if I waited for him to revel in the offering of my heart.

I only wanted to know if *The Current Squeeze* was truly interested in me or passing the time until something better came along—or worse still—hung up on issues I couldn't escape; an ex-girlfriend— a festering wound from his past.

Well, to be blunt, I made the decision not to wait for an indecisive prick. I took the bull by the proverbial horns and told him what I had planned; jungle surfing on a zip-line through the rainforest. He was keen, but I had to negotiate attendance with a drive-thru breakfast. I should have gone alone.

By the time we arrived, I'd subjected him to two hours of bad Karaoke, one oozing road kill and a bucket-load of awkward conversation. The upside? While we dined on Tuna wraps and toasted sandwiches in scintillating silence, *The Cockney* had messaged me for a brief, humorous chat.

I told him about my impending death via zip-line and that the local arachnid populace may have been genetically altered, biological weapons created by the government given their size and menace. He said I should kiss my ass goodbye regarding flying through the tree canopy and take my chances with the spiders. We ended the conversation there; *The Current Squeeze* had finished his sandwich and now vied for attention.

We decided a brief, romantic walk was in order. We had forty minutes to kill and the encroaching spiders were more than we could handle without a flamethrower. We walked hand-in-hand along the beach—the first physical contact of the day. It inspired sand drawings of silly love hearts filled with our initials. He promptly informed me the rising tide would eradicate our musings.

Kill joy.

My mood took a nosedive. Rain started sheeting down, upholding the Rainforest's reputation for damp conditions. My hair became a disaster and notions of premature death were bought to the fore when a stoner in a minivan picked us up for jungle surfing with a joint still splitting his crusty, dry lips.

Ugh.

He mounted every pothole like a dog on heat and even made a side trip to the convenient store for chocolate which he failed to share. At least the trip to the zip line entrance was short, but fucking bumpy! I was impressed the tree-hugger kept the van on the road and I didn't wet my pants.

The wet weather and the fact I smelt like an ashtray soon was forgotten; being kitted in safety vests, harnesses and hard hats quickly reminded me of the fun we were supposedly going to have.

I was dubbed 'Wonder Woman' due to my swollen chest measurements and dark, unfortunately moisture-ridden curling tangle of locks. And, since I needed a little cheering up, I assigned *The Current Squeeze* with the hard hat labelled: 'Princess Leia'. He wasn't impressed, though I thought it a riot and somewhat well deserved.

Jungle surfing was not what I expected. Endless talks about native flora and fauna did my head in and having to wait for each individual person to be trussed in safety equipment between stops saw my overactive imagination pushing people over the edge of the platforms.

I delighted in opportunities to hang upside down or careen the zip-line at high speed, but since said experiences were few and far between, I ended up cold and bored.

My happy moment for the day was as surprising as the feather light caress upon my fingertips. *The Current Squeeze* ordained me with a gesture that was innocent and intimate, leaning close to whisper in my ear sweet nothings. I smiled widely from the touch of his skin against mine.

I'd like to say that the minor contact led to other amorous activities, but sadly, we went our separate ways at the end of the day. We had our own personal lives, friends, family and absolutely no idea how to combine them.

I heard that he'd played on the beach with sticks of fire and miraculously didn't kill anyone. I went to *The Bestie's* house, drank half a bottle of suspicious looking alcohol and had promptly fallen asleep on the floor.

Good times.

Day Six

*T*oday I put Martha Stewart to shame with my domestic goddess prowess. I knitted a full length woollen sofa-throw, built a dining room table from licence plates and decided to turn my car into a luxury motor home. I was elbow deep in cotton thread, pressed metal and supple leather for half the morning before I realised I was over-achieving.

That was bullshit.

I was really elbow-deep in disinfectant and toilet scum—having scrubbed the apartment from top to bottom and laundered every dirty sheet. Swathes of Egyptian cotton were strewn across unmanned appliances and various pieces of furniture; I was too much of a cheapskate to invest in a dryer. The sense of accomplishment was immense, but my levels of boredom skyrocketed.

At least I had something to look forward to, well, I had something to overanalyse and probably vilify by day's end. I planned to introduce *The Current Squeeze* to the menagerie.

To most it might sound rather ordinary; images of Sunday roasts, Yorkshire puddings and innocent laughs. In most cases this would be the usual highlight reel from dinner with *The Family*, but crazy was not simply a state of mind in our household. *The Mother* was possibly going senile, drank far too much wine and would undoubtedly be asleep on the sofa by seven. *The Father* was addicted to his smart phone, lesbian porn and eating marmalade with eggs. As for *The Siblings*? They swore like dirty sailors and had a fetish for showing the world their ass cracks.

The Bestie was coming for morale support—not because I was ashamed of my crazy relations (I actually applauded our eccentricities)—to offer a secondary set of arms should *The Current Squeeze* try to bolt again. On two separate occasions he'd bailed on this meeting. That was a sign—a sign that I was probably dating a dick.

The entourage began a little after four-thirty. I drove everyone despite desperate urges to rob a liquor store and hide the loot in my stomach lining. *The Current Squeeze* had similar notions, already nursing a half bottle of amber liquid to his lips while two empties sat prone in his lap.

He winked when he saw my crest-fallen face. He resembled a twitchy pirate; one shuttered eyelid barely making it open again. I knew then we were all in for a splendid night.

<Insert sarcasm here>.

I hustled him into the car, another bottle of beer in hand as he assured me that his nerves were a fading memory—so was his concise speech and ability to walk in a straight line, but pointing that out would not sober him up.

I then drove like a maniac to *The Bestie's* house. Reckless ducking and weaving through Sunday drivers, incessant horn blasts and erect middle fingers were the salute to my bitumen fury. I cared not for tickets or twisted metal; my mind had become a flurry of unwanted activity and I needed my wing-woman stat!

With the luggage of all companions by my side, I soon stood outside the family home, knuckles poised against the timber door, unmoving. Was this a defining moment? Were the scales of judgment set in motion, the weighted opinion of my loved ones the ultimate decider whether my love-life proceeded forward or abruptly ended?

The awkward moments faded into a background of hard and fast handshakes and forced smiles. He mingled, laughed at *The Father's* fart jokes and kept his eyebrows lowered at *The Mother's* inebriated barrage of relationship questions. He could have also been falling asleep.

With a few more beers under his belt and quick trip to the

balcony to smoke weed with *The Siblings*, *The Family* accepted him, but were not sold on him either. The cloud of chronic fumes mattered little. *The Father* believed I deserved better than I seemingly settled for.

Despite *The Mother's* acquaintance with the toilet bowl that night and *The Father's* wise words, I was surprised how much I had enjoyed myself. *The Family* were just plain good value even if *The Current Squeeze* had let me down more than I care to mention.

Day Seven

*M*onday's blow! A short statement, but never a truer one spoken, except for perhaps: Monday's bite the big one, Monday's can suck it and Monday's can go get fisted!

The painful anticipation of five working days ahead coupled with the inescapable obligation to pay bills put a major dampener on the start of the week. Praying for a sugar-daddy was an option, but hardly practical.

Fantasies of the easy life were easily indulged, especially when coupled with what could surely be labelled the most boring day in history. Watching paint dry was more scintillating. The few scattered laughs I had partaken were surely a fluke.

The Boss disappeared a little after ten; she was neck deep in a spew bag and stumbling in the car park like a drunken hobo. I felt bad about the glee I felt in her misfortune; her exit meant I could abuse my second-in-command privileges.

I promptly sent two co-workers home. I may have been bored and stuck at work, but the others could leave, max credit cards at department stores or run children over in unmanned school zones. That just left me and *The Bestie* to research anal beads on the internet and plank on the front counter.

Yes. It didn't need to be said. We should have been working. We should have answered the phone and probably shouldn't have set fire to the staff room, but it was Monday and Monday could go and fist itself!

When the clock struck five, I slammed the reception door home and rolled my wagon out of there, cruising home as fast as the car would take me. Between speed (the moving tyre variety) and the cranked up tunes pumping through my speakers, I bore a smile wider than an elephant's ass.

It had been a bloody boring day, but no one had died, *The Bestie* and I hadn't had to pay to repair the fire damage (mostly because we wouldn't admit to arson) and now because I'd found my peaceful zone, was listening to music and singing badly.

I chased good tracks and a dangerous drive home with a safe walk on the beach. 'Safe' was definable only on whether or not the lifeguards were mutant and now impaled people with their swim flags or whether or not jellyfish had grown go-go-gadget tentacles to capture and suck me into a watery grave.

Neither tragic event occurred as the sand squelched beneath my toes and the water lapped my ankles. I might have seen a killer lap-dog poised to attack a fallen coconut, but his vicious claws were buffered by ridiculous pink socks.

Today was not the most glamorous or interesting start to the week, but it was certainly the most positive way to end the beginning. I found some solace on the beach front while blowing my ear drums with pop music; I figured this constituted the very definition of Monday bliss.

I hoped to find a similar source of happiness on each approaching day. It cost nothing, but instilled calm—a favourable result. Tuesday could only be a step up from here.

Day Eight

*T*oday sucked balls. There was no other way to put it. After Monday's savage attempt to rob me of my sense of humour and tragically force boredom upon me, I had no idea how Tuesday could inspire me to take a tyre iron to my face. Monotony never ceased and crazy thoughts ran rampant. All forms of logic were repelled as I attempted to leash negative thoughts. Doubt was a silent killer and crept over me with foreboding relentlessness; I predicted that something bad was going to happen and soon.

What made it more pitiable? The absolute best part of my day was the rickety, unpolished clock mounted upon the cracked plaster wall striking five, an indication that the end to forced pleasantness had fallen upon me.

I was truly melancholy and had no real idea as to why. I was in a mood seemingly unredeemable, the kind of disposition that made me wish my worst enemies wiped their ass with a cheese grater and that my sleazy neighbour would repeatedly slam his head in a car door.

Exercise didn't help. The power of the endorphin rush was a lie Yoga instructors peddled so I'd come back to class despite hamstring injuries and bilious gas released during spread-eagle poses. So even though I skipped mantras in lieu of pounding out a five kilometre circuit and discussing boys with *The Bestie*, it still was not enough to shake the funk.

She tried everything to bring me back from the darkened recesses of my overactive imagination, but I'd already set up camp there and now wallowed in the ominous weight of the unknown that pressed upon me.

I chased exercise and pointless chatter with a protein shake for dinner; it did nothing to improve my temperament. In fact, the only thing that lifted the edges of my downturned lips was a text from *The Current Squeeze*, asking about my day.

I told him that I'd found an Irish leprechaun under a rainbow who'd pooped a pot of gold that I'd spent on strippers and cider, but he was unmoved. He never did ask what was wrong, but made the effort to cheer me up, messaging the ridiculous lyrics from the 'Don't Worry be Happy' song.

I chased the brief interlude with lacklustre television that invited me to learn how to sharpen my kitchen knives and how to cook apple turnovers with Chantilly cream.

Not exactly scintillating stuff.

I was about to hit the hay and write off this uneventful day as 'tragic' when I started receiving inappropriate texts from an old lover. Perfect; just what I wanted before bed. He was more likely to have a pineapple shoved backwards up his rear end before I ever let him see me naked again.

I fended him off, said goodnight to the world and hid under the blankets for the rest of the evening. It was warm, quiet and surprisingly peaceful between the crisp, cotton sheets.

As I drifted off, I hoped Wednesday would not be a repeat of the previous two days. I also contemplated the logistics of pineapple placement in a man's posterior and fell asleep trying to problem solve the spiny green leaf arrangement.

Day Nine

*W*hen I thought about uneventful days in the past, they looked like this one—mediocre. A work day like any other, I was busy with the business of congeniality and patience. I answered phones and solved problems, took money from the reluctant and smiled in kind at the pained.

I was overwhelmed by how ordinary some days could be and how claiming a slither of happiness amongst everything already known could be tiresome. In fact, I couldn't remember anything that melted my icy exterior or brought a smile to my lips. My eyes were glazed like a sugared donut, moving on occasion only to observe what appeared to be unmoving clock hands.

Wait … There was something that made me laugh; an incident that any bored employee would throw their head back in uncontrollable amusement. How could I have almost forgotten the only part of my day that saw me pee my pants just a little?

The story begins like any other, deep in the haunted woods … Red Riding Hood was throwing rocks at the Big Bad Wolf and calling him a pussy, while grandma planted magic mushrooms for the illustrious Hansel and Gretel. Last time those crazy drug addicts ventured north, they bragged about a gingerbread house and some hoarder witch with a hefty broomstick collection. Grandma thought they were filthy little liars, but she was old and unaware her garden was a breeding ground for hallucinogenics.

Um … yeah …

Clearly I need to stop trippin' through the garden, too.

Anyway, back to the vinyl chair and melamine counter in which I actually resided.

The roller seat was my usual post in which I toiled the day away while my fingers whirred across the keypad for data entry. It wasn't the least bit thrilling until—cue horror music—the phone rang.

'Thank you for calling my shithole job, you're speaking with a ninja assassin,' I'd respectfully said.

'Hi, Ninja Assassin, I'm calling back to discuss the results of my pap smear.'

At this point I paused, scratched the bridge of my nose, and felt the beginning of a smile touch the corners of my lips; one—because I'd been referred to as a ninja assassin and two—a stranger wanted to talk about vaginas.

'Pap smear results?' I'd repeated. 'I think you might have the wrong end of the speculum.'

'Oh, so I haven't called 'Swab my Hooha'?'

'No, you've called 'My Shithole Job'.'

'I'm so sorry, Ninja Assassin.'

'No problems,' I'd said, biting my tongue and any future eruption of laughter, 'Good luck with your discharge.'

As I hung up the phone, I laughed until my stomach surrendered lunch. It was worth the acid reflux finding humour and just a skerrick of happiness assembled from a conversation with a confused syphilis carrier. What else had I smiled about lately?

Day Ten

"Another turning point, a fork stuck in the road. Time grabs you by the hand directs you where to go." – Greenday.

A lyric that spoke the truth—or rather—exemplified my life-to-date. So many changes had occurred over the last year alone; the collapse of my marriage and the celebration of good times with friends. I'd partied and self-pitied, rolled around in new bed sheets and explored options for an uncertain future. I'd laughed, cried and … loved.

Love was the seed of a flower I'd never seen take hold in the garden of my youth. It had suddenly bloomed, golden in its manifestation and completely unexpected. I hadn't understood the emotion instilled at the time. I'd had no idea what to do with it or how to deal with its presence. I'd only known that the love had come from friendship and a fierce need to protect; different to what I searched for now. The love I'd felt then had eventually become awkward, but never anything I since regretted.

This love—my marriage—ended and everything changed. Love had become a word held closer to the chest than a hand of poker and ironically not even my biggest concern for the future. Financial hardship now plagued my thoughts. I'd gone from a double income and a life of comfort to trying to rub two cents together. I'd never had to fend for myself until now and although I managed rather well, sometimes I felt like throwing myself at the mercy of the welfare system.

I shouldn't have hastily slapped a pair of E-cups on my flat and sorry excuse for a chest, but it was my one and only post-divorce gift to myself; surgery was a chance to turn my pancakes with nipples into something with curves, femininity and relative size! It restored the confidence I'd lost and certainly aided with my sexual agenda, too.

One life, no regrets; a mantra I had tattooed on my forearm to remember the notion. I tried desperately to apply the expression to the extravagant purchase of silicone. Two maxed out credit cards, minimum wage income and the niggling doubt that when financial freedom finally came, I'd realise I was still single, loveless and sporting an inflatable chest as a consolation prize.

One plus side? Temporary lack of funds meant groceries were a luxury. Tinned tuna and pickles were a staple, water was now classified as wine and since I was half-starved, the empty cupboards also rivalled most weight loss programs. I was also slightly malnourished and had turned mildly yellow, but that was a story for another day.

The truth was that I spent a lot of time worrying if I could afford to have coffee with my friends, bail *The Siblings* out of prison when they might need it or *The Current Squeeze* hiding his wallet in disgust while shaking his head at me. I also thought about world peace and the logistics of midget porn, but I didn't rate them quite as highly on the care-factor scale.

The pressure finally got to me today and I had a breakdown; the emotional kind where I leak more than a pipe and collect ungodly amounts of snot in my nose and throat.

I was trying to execute my job with a degree of finesse; carving up bodies for the city morgue and selling the parts on the black market to crazy cannibals in South America was not an easy task. It was a competitive market now that the North Koreans were involved, but I do my best. The problem wasn't the excessive blood or the fact that the bone saw was blunter than a butter knife; it was the sadness setting in again, something I couldn't shake, but tried to ignore.

The Bestie could see I was a little down and thought reminding me about our late-night shopping venture would perk me up, but since my financial status only lent itself to window shopping, I knew I'd be a killjoy.

Two other co-workers decided to join us—the more the merrier—but when a fine dining experience was added to a night where I couldn't afford socks, I lost my shit.

Tears welled and my nose buzzed with building emotion. The frenzy within grew exponentially and rushed towards all exits to erupt from the pressure cooker that was my body. I barely got away from the counter before wet saltiness spilled down my cheeks like a rupturing volcano.

I tasted the agonising despair on my tongue—bitter like my mood. I cried so hard I could barely breathe. Gasping, I tried desperately to get the outburst under control; this wasn't me. I never lost control; I'd always been contained. It made life easier in the past.

The unforseen moment spewed heightened emotion from every orifice. My applecart had finally toppled. I didn't even realise I had a freaking applecart. When had I become a fruit vender? What would I do with all the ruined merchandise?

There were a million things I took for granted, lacked or couldn't reclaim since the divorce. There were also a million more things I didn't understand, couldn't afford or simply longed for that couldn't be accomplished.

I was tired, confused by the concept of dating again, affected constantly by the judgement of those around me, unhappy with my job and in desperate need of a holiday. It was in that moment of weakness I felt everything crash upon me; a self-made wreck.

My first world problems were not going to solve themselves. I had to put my big girl panties on, stop bloody crying and unearth some damn happiness. How could I find this elusive emotion, move forward, plaster a smile upon my face and carry on with so much still unresolved?

I couldn't.

The Boss sent me packing and made me promise to take the rest of the weekend to think clearly about what I truly wanted. Her advice was golden. I had to stop hoping for a life I didn't actually have and enjoy the present. Everything had changed, but common sense should still remain; pay bills, relax about dating, spend time with friends and find serenity in solitude.

I decided to sit down and re-assess not just my financial outlook, but emotional and work related one, too. I started with my secret stash of funds. I conquered the mounting bills, reworked my budget, found extra money for savings, holidays and approximately three lines of cocaine.

Kidding. It was only two.

I decided to play it cool with the dating gig. *The Current Squeeze* was hard to read, but I figured he must like me. Surely he wouldn't keep calling or coming around if he didn't; unless I just was that good in bed?

Yes, the road was often unpaved and difficult to navigate—and yes—some days I want to fall in a heap and give up, but in the end, *The Boss* had made her point.

'Live the life you have and make it grand'.

I'll always smile for the truth in that statement if nothing else. Oh and because of the three lines of cocaine, too.

Day Eleven

*A*fter yesterday's mini-emotional breakdown, it was fair to say that my puffy eyes did not appear behind the melamine counter at work today. I looked as if I'd been thrown into the midst of a wasp's nest—the resultant swelling of too many tears. I'd had to put ice-packs on my face just so *The Current Squeeze* would recognize me.

Vanity aside, lack of income continued to play havoc with my mind; taking yet another day off work depleted the earnings pile, but I forced myself to ignore building alarm as I'd recalculated my budget and was not as financially destitute as I first believed.

This morning I woke up early to indulge *The Current Squeeze*; he'd spent the night, his warm body pressed comfortingly against mine, his arms wrapped tightly around me. I courted the idea that we'd spooned all night because the sight of my swollen face was still unsettling; I'd never know.

He grumbled as I bounded out of bed, but was soon distracted by the overzealous dedication to his craft. Photography was his speciality and he had plans to capture the torrential winds of a cyclone on course to cross the coast sometime later that night.

As long-time locals, neither of us were bothered by the cyclone's looming presence; we would only panic if the bright stadium lights of the local football field were set for collision or the shopping centre ran out of the three C's: canned beans, candles and condoms.

The Current Squeeze wanted to document the callous nature of said winds and the roaring ocean currents at my local beach. He also asked to capture me in this dangerous photo shoot, but since my face still looked like a semi-trailer had left skid marks on it, he wisely concentrated on the nature angle instead.

Tagging along meant I became a victim of the freezing cold and was battered by wayward spray. I appreciated his passion and was impressed by the dedication his efforts depicted, but curling back up in bed was infinitely more appealing.

Hours spent battling the disgraceful weather outside saw us indulge a nice, warm shower after returning home—not together—very much separate. I soaped alone while he dicked around with his camera, editing the morning's work and grunting periodically.

The Cockney sent a message while I was washing sea spray from my hair. He asked if I'd stocked up on beans and candles before the encroaching storm blew in. He also warned against eating the beans, farting and then lighting matches in the same room; solid advice.

He never mentioned condoms.

After the shower, I cooked breakfast, avoided canned legumes and pottered around the apartment. *The Cockney* and I continued sending harmless messages back and forth. It was nice to talk to someone with a decent sense of humour; he too was unconcerned by the weather and had even contemplated a little pre-storm lark on his jet ski.

I offered him some solid advice—wear a life jacket and take a flare gun!

The Current Squeeze eventually noticed my inattention and decided to leave. It was a good thing. I was strangely itching to indulge my creative juices and start writing … something; he was a distraction.

I hadn't felt compelled to execute my craft in quite a while. There'd been so many mental roadblocks I unwittingly erected to repel my usual addiction to the written word. I started to wonder if I'd ever write a plot twist, italicise an expletive or laugh at my own poo jokes again. Maybe because I'd watched *The Current Squeeze* absorbed in a world of apertures and shutter speeds I recognised that I too had once been passionate about something important.

It bugged me that it had taken someone else to show me that.

I wrote consistently for several hours, editing my tidings and exploring passions long forgotten. It was decidedly freeing to feel creativity flow through my veins again, to have the urge to express thoughts with swift keystrokes, but the cyclone was on its way and my apartment was located in flood territory—evacuation paramount. I was even hustled by *The Mother* to get my ass into gear and over to *The Current Squeeze's* place before becoming land-locked by rising water. I relented even though I wasn't quite ready to let the morning's progress pass.

A party was on the agenda for the evening. The guest list? Three. It was a horrid substitute for the birthday bash I actually had planned and cancelled thanks to cyclone 'fucking inconvenient', but at least I'd be entertained through the blustery weather.

I stocked up on cider because beer tasted like goat urine and wine made me spew more than a fifth grader on sugar. I headed out, popped the bottle caps as soon as I arrived and prayed the night would be stocked with laughter, wicked naughty sex, and then more sex because I just really, really liked it.

By midnight I was drunk; too many shots were consumed, guitars had been strummed indecently and I smoked enough pot that swinging the neighbour's cat by the tail seemed more like a fun game than animal abuse. By one o'clock I abandoned all activities in lieu of locating *The Current Squeeze*. He'd disappeared thirty minutes earlier; turns out he wasn't desecrating the bathroom, but rather, passed out in bed.

All hopes of wicked, naughty sex were dashed. Happiness evaporated and bitter disappointment was the pill I had to swallow. I showered and headed to bed myself, hoping that the morning would awaken a boyfriend excited to be with me in any way possible.

Day Twelve

Cyclones were not only dangerous, but exciting. They could reduce homes to rubble in the blink of an eye, but mostly brought families and friends closer as common fear and pending disaster marked the air with uncertainty. Destructive winds, swollen creeks, splintering trees and lack of power contributed to the need to be together.

Trapped was my word to describe it; forced moments of intimacy, laughter and conversation ruled the agenda. It was the perfect opportunity to reconnect with those I might otherwise brush aside on a daily basis or take for granted.

I was trapped with *The Current Squeeze* and his family; a happy coincidence since I actually like them. They'd welcomed me into their home and their hearts, opened their doors to my transient appearances and fed me on more occasions than *The Current Squeeze* himself had. They were warm, honest and didn't mind when I drank all their coffee and raided the kid's lolly jar. They didn't even mind when I kicked a golf ball into the windscreen of their car or the time I'd taken out their letterbox with my rear bumper. They were just fun, forgiving people; today offered no exception.

The cyclone had left mass flooding on a property that presented with hilly slopes and opportunities for mayhem. It was only natural that old bits of plywood surfaced and we all dangerously skimboarded our way into legend.

I hadn't had that much fun in ages. You couldn't label me the next skim board champion, but I put in a good effort, stowed my natural fear and concentrated on the laughter of those around me. I even ignored my constant suction and the clumps of grass and mud that had taken up residence in my pants.

Childish fun subsided; the adults were left to contemplate conversation and each other; a little bit of cabin fever had begun to set in. Something was wrong with *The Current Squeeze*, the mud sliding did nothing to retract his sombre mood. I wasn't sure if his behaviour stemmed from seeing me three days running or because we were trapped.

Locked in location by floodwaters, I offered to leave regardless. Some roads had to have been open and I didn't like the feeling that crept over me; this strange sensation of not being wanted. In fact, if I was one hundred percent honest, I'd been feeling it for quite some time. He was too quiet, distracted and more distant than my apartment in the next suburb, but what could I do? Annoy him with questions? Batter him with my insecurities until he told me what I wanted to hear rather than the truth?

No.

He must have sensed my urgency and tried to explain everything despite my self-protect instincts kicking in. The more he tried, the more I pulled away—my only option to avoid further pain. He promised everything was in order and that he was perfectly happy in my presence, but I knew better.

I should have run then. I should have listened to my instincts, battled floodwaters and got the hell out of that relationship.

Awkwardness slithered over both of us. We watched movies, barely touched, and avoided the inevitability of bed. I was suddenly terrified to be alone with him and I could only imagine what was going through his head.

We made love that night, but I knew in my heart of hearts that it was for the very last time. Every caress was tentative and shaky, every kiss uncertain and clumsy. I remember looking deep into his eyes and reading hesitant desire; the reflection of my growing feelings were not mirrored. He still clung to the past and a woman who'd left him broken and unable to move forward with someone new—someone like me.

The real truth then came out. I still have no idea what prompted him to speak, but I never spoke, merely listened. I wanted clarity despite words not being his strong suit and consequently, my heart ached from the reality check I received.

I'd made a grave mistake. I'd started to fall in love with him, something I never planned on happening. He was a distraction and a ploy to engage the touch of a man again. I'd wanted to frolic with someone who shared similar interests—someone who I planned on seeing only temporarily. I'd ruined everything by allowing my guard to fall and my heart to accept someone clearly emotionally unavailable.

I refused to cry. I refused to let him hear or see that I was damaged by his admissions. His unrelenting attraction to me was irrelevant; our blossoming romance was now in tatters, lost amongst the memory of the crinkled bed sheets beside us.

I had a fitful sleep that night, wondering how I'd allowed myself to fall into such a mess. I'd become a consolation prize, second best and forever doomed to walk in the shadow of his ex. I didn't want to be anything less than someone's everything.

In that moment I wished I was a bird so I could fly far, far away—fly to happiness and leave behind the mistakes of today…

Day Thirteen

*M*y eyes sprang open a little after sunrise. Light streamed through the open window and balcony door, warming the sheets in which I laid. Continued sleep was impossible—not that I'd had any. So much swam through my mind. I'd solved little with my bumbling inner dialogue. My eyes were now open and I could finally see what I'd missed from the start.

I rolled over. The chiselled body nestled next to me was etched quickly into my memory with the carving tools of my mind. He slept soundly, mouth slightly ajar, the lines on his face eased by the comfort of sleep or perhaps it was the release of last night's burden.

My stomach rolled with a sickness I'd never quite known. It was the knowledge; I could never retrace my steps and go back to a time when I hadn't been so careless. My feelings were stronger than I realised and though I'd done everything to avoid them, I'd failed. I'd started to fall for this complex man and I was bitterly alone in the sentiment.

I crawled out of bed, careful to avoid waking him. I needed to think and quickly; I needed to come up with a suitable exit strategy, something unachievable without drinking bucket loads of black brew.

A part of me hoped he'd realise the potential in our union and confess he was blinded by a past that wasn't coming back to claim him. I knew, of course, that was never going to happen. I'd been living in a fantasy world that I needed to evacuate.

I'd barely finished my coffee when *The Current Squeeze* joined me in the kitchen. He was strange in his efforts to be bright and cheery, touching and reassuring me that he wanted me and only me. I'd never felt so uncomfortable in his arms or less certain of his promises.

Post-divorce, this was my second chance at life and an opportunity to meet someone who wanted to be my everything without exception. So, why the hell would I want to settle for second best when I deserved to be happy in requited love?

I swallowed my pride, plastered a fake smile on my face and temporarily accepted his proclamations until I figured out exactly how I would end this.

He suggested a drive to inspect the cyclone damage; I needed to see if my car could traverse whatever over-the-road water may have remained. Was escape plausible? Would my 'adult' status be revoked by running away?

Alas, the drive proved I was still stranded to some extent.

Defeated and biting back repressed tears, he reached for me. He stroked my back and told me to ignore his admissions from the previous night; claimed his words were confused, not well considered and not entirely accurate of his thoughts and feelings in the light of the new day.

My heart wanted to find solace in his repenting, but I'd had enough. He lightly kissed my lips, told me that I was wonderful, but only managed to water those seeds of nefarious self-doubt further. I then did what the coward in me had begged for hours— ran—I ran as fast as my legs would carry me. I threw my stuff in the car and bolted down his driveway like the devil himself was chasing me with a pitchfork.

Within minutes of the great escape my phone rang ... and rang. I ignored his call and wondered why he'd chosen that moment to chase me when he'd had four months to realise my worth. What was it about endings that prompted the responses we longed for at the beginning?

I eventually pulled over. I was driving like Batman on the roads of Gotham—dangerously and without fear. It didn't bother me that I side-swiped a mini-van and ran over a pedestrian that looked suspiciously like *The Boss*. I was blinded by the sting of tears I'd thus far refused to release.

I took a shallow breath, shook it off as best as I could and headed to the only place I could access—*The Parent's* house. Naturally they comforted me and offered advice. I knew that in order to get past the damage threatening to crush my heart, I had to find some way to move forward and quickly.

It was unfathomable finding happiness that day—unless Jason Statham knocked on the front door wearing nothing but a smile, held a jar of chocolate sauce and promised to lick it clean from my naked body—so I wallowed in the land of sadness.

Another lesson learned.

I wasn't sure of the lesson's future results, but I figured all would be revealed when the full brunt of the day's events unfolded. I only knew that I could no longer look back and hope for something that might have been. The path in front was unknown and scary, but I imagined that letting go meant that something truly amazing would propel me forward into a future worth investigating. After all, I didn't have eyes in the front of my head to keep looking backwards.

Day Fourteen

*M*onday—the day after my cowardly bolt. There was no significance to the day other than the fact I'd come to think of my mind as a Rubik's cube; everything was so far out of alignment.

When things got crazy in the brain vault—as they were on this day—I turned to exercise. I threw on my joggers, hoping to climb a mountain, kill my calves and then get smashed by an oncoming vehicle before my lungs collapsed.

Neither happened; it was just a workout.

I occupied my scatterbrain with errant thoughts of riding mechanical bulls as my thighs chaffed and I puffed like a geriatric. Such silly thoughts had something to do with craving tacos; which led to thoughts of meat; progressed to cattle and concluded with me wondering if I'd look good in chaps.

I never did reach a conclusion.

Responsibility loomed. *The Boss* (who I hadn't run down with my car the previous day), had started her vacation. Translation: Step up, fill her shoes and run the work show while she was away. No one cared about my problems, thus professionalism was a must, especially when I felt so …

I found no pleasure in today. In fact, I wasn't certain I'd find pleasure in any upcoming days, but there were moments. I concentrated on smiling, attending to every last detail and ensuring everyone else was happy. It was my mission statement at the beginning of this journey to bring out the best in others even if I couldn't do it for myself.

One hundred happy days—or at least the concept of it—was more than a selfish notion. It had to be about finding positivity in others and situations presented. I chose to look upon each day as an opportunity to make another person feel brighter about themselves—in other words—the gift of joy offered to another should be cherished as a gift unto itself. Unbelievably, I managed to spread good cheer despite feeling as if I'd harpooned a pod of whales.

After work, I headed home. It was the first time I'd returned to the apartment since the cyclone and the front room was flooded. I took a deep breath, screamed just a little, said words like 'shit' and 'fuck' and then considered kicking a chair through the front window. I refrained, grabbed a bucket and mop and proceeded to sponge up the weather's debris; all accomplished while moaning like a goat with its ass on fire.

By the time the last of the water was cleared, my throat was hoarse from empty complaints and exhaustion finally overcame me. All I wanted to do in that moment was sit down and write. I wanted to expel all thoughts and renew a vigour I used to have for the written word. I also wanted to lick peanut butter off a Calvin Klein model's chest, but I was too tired and overly dour.

I ate directly from the peanut butter jar instead.

Day Fifteen

Slithers of flamingo pink ruptured the sky, bursting through the darkened corridor of a horizon that laid claim to morning. The night had died, taking a final breath that expelled stars into a receding darkness that would no doubt return at a later time. A new day had awakened and with it, a dawn so magnificent you had to see it to believe it.

On this morning I stood in my living room, clutching my coffee mug as I gazed out the window. The apartment was silent bar the sound of my breath and the steady beat of what I imagined might be my broken heart.

In that moment the pain was numbed by what my eyes bared witness—colours—a sky so infinite and resplendent that misery was temporarily forgotten. It was breathtaking. I immersed myself in another zone, another time, and what I hoped might be an alternate reality.

I promptly dropped my dirty dishes in the sink, gathered my belongings for work and headed out while the inclination to bathe in magnificence was strong. I arrived at the beachfront within minutes, slammed the car door behind me and chased the sunrise to the edge of a rocky outcrop.

Waves crashed all around me and the salty breeze teased the tangled thatch of my curling hair. I didn't care. I craved only beauty in that moment; a representation of the very beginning of time and the promise of eternal days dripping in vibrant hues of bliss.

I wanted to linger indefinitely, soaking up the essence of God's masterpiece, but time was against me and work was an unavoidable reality. I had to lay tracks and leave beauty in the rear view mirror. The almighty dollar beckoned and so did my phone; a message from *The Cockney* flashed across the screen.

'How are you?' he'd asked me.

What could I say? That I was just dandy? And no, I wasn't bothered by the current state of my love life?

He didn't know. In fact, he had no idea I'd even had a 'current squeeze'. *The Cockney* and I discussed nothing more than life and its nuisances and everything else in between. Ironically, he was everything I expected a good man to appear; interested, but not pushy; intelligent, but not arrogant. Attractive? Well, I assumed he might be based on his stellar personality and witty charm, but I honestly had no idea. We were only pen-pals.

I never bothered responding to his question. I knew it was rude, but I didn't have a pleasant answer and he definitely deserved more than my sour mood. He didn't deserve my silence either, but what did the faceless man who randomly messaged me expect me to provide?

More than I could give at the time.

Arriving at my shithole job; everyone was in a frightfully good mood. It helped more than I realised. I wasn't capable of shaking thoughts of negligence regarding the relationship I'd bolted from. Happy dispositions were an excellent distraction, but I still wondered; would today be the day he contacted me? Would he ever contact me again and really, did I want him to?

The day passed quickly. By four o'clock I faded and opted to head out early to attend a beauty appointment. I'd like to say it was a special treat—a way to perk myself up—it wasn't fun. Hair was brutally zapped from every orifice; a modern form of torture that the masochist in me craved. At least after I was tasered and lasered I had my esplanade walk with *The Bestie* to look forward to.

The flashing blue light on my phone made an appearance, taunting and teasing me while I wondered if the popcorn smell that continued to waft from under my armpits came with a frozen coke and ice-cream cone.

The Ex-Squeeze had contacted me.

I thought I'd feel relieved, excited or awkward—none of which I felt. A massive part of me hoped the message would be filled with regret and longing, but alas, it was a spiel crafted from badly strung bullshit; filled with tales of my apparent beauty, grace and winning personality. After several complimentary, translucent sentences, he explained his state of numbness and that he'd become void of the ability to connect emotionally with anyone since his Ex.

'Can we still be friends?' he'd asked me.

Fuck off.

Maybe …

It didn't take long to conjure up images of a rhinoceros going Serengeti on his ass and taking him up the back door with his ivory. To suggest friendship after the places his tongue had been was just plain weird. How could I allow this man to start burrowing his way deeper into my feelings?

An act of bravery—or stupidity—forced me to dial his number. He answered on the second ring, voice hoarse. I wanted no promises for tomorrow; just clarification and bitter finality. We were done and I'd accelerated the end by fleeing from a situation I'd unconsciously decided there'd be no resolution.

Had I done the right thing?

It was a resounding yes. It didn't matter that in that moment an assault rifle was fired at my chest; flesh torn open and blood splattered in every direction, but I saved myself from a second shot. I was heavily wounded from this invisible attack, but I knew to push any dark emotions down as deep as the pit would allow, praying the implosion never begged release.

I terminated the conversation quickly. It had become cyclic and all evidence suggested that confusion was apparent from every angle. There was nothing to gain trying to salvage something clearly lacking substance. An emotional web still held him captive and I was done with the stickiness of any lingering hurt.

The Bestie knew something was wrong the minute she saw me. I barely said two words of explanation for my tardiness when one final message appeared on my phone.

'I don't want to lose you and what we started, okay? That much I know for sure. XX'.

Fuck off.

Maybe …

What could I do with that information? I'd already affirmed that I'd never be a consolation prize again and wouldn't allow exception now because he was emotionally retarded! The only thing certain was that I couldn't break down. I absolutely one hundred and ten percent forbade myself from crying. In my mind it was considered completely unacceptable.

So I raised my chin, plastered a smile across my face and opted for steely resolve.

I did not falter.

I did not show weakness, but continued to hope. Could happiness be found in that?

Day Sixteen

Wow—rough day!

Fancy having gone to work when I was certain there was a gaping hole in my chest where my heart should've been. Could no one see it? Did no one think to call emergency services when they'd seen nothing but an empty shell?

Suck it up princess.

I repeated those words in my head again and again; a mantra I hoped would cure me of this ridiculous sadness. If not, I could swallow a bag of rapid-set concrete and either; die a horrendous death via lime poisoning or harden the fuck up.

With so much poverty, famine, war and oppression in the world, what right did I have to feel tormented over what could be considered a trivial matter of the heart? Yes, every breath felt like the last and I ached with a fierceness I can't really describe, but falling apart and releasing a cascade of pointless tears would solve nothing. Mascara would run, I'd resemble a panda, be captured by a Chinese zoo keeper and shoved in a four foot glass box and fed bamboo for the rest of my life.

So, I decided to ignore wayward feelings for as long as humanly possible and live in the magical world of denial; functioning was a necessity. I needed to remember to eat, exercise, pay bills and smile at people I'd labelled friends—oh and look at adding more fibre to my diet. Toilet time had not been fun lately.

Anyway …

Today I laughed. It surprised the hell out of me. I won't say it made me happy, but it stretched my drooped lips in another direction; a pleasant change from tripping over them. The deplorable morals of social networkers made me crack; their ridiculously low standards and endless pursuit of the drunken selfie to blame.

I never browsed social media sites to coo over kiddy photos, lick my lips at dinner snapshots or gush over fucking ugly cats! I was a voyeur of naughty humour, travel porn and hot blokes.

Today was no exception as I rummaged through posts like: would you tap this; photos of obese women in crazy outfits with too much spandex. I also snorted at E-cards and the various use of graphic language. I inspected posts regarding newborns and probably thought they were too chubby. That cutsie photo taken of husbands in heinous sweaters knitted at Christmas crossed my mind as better doused in gasoline and set on fire.

What really got me going was a photo of a giant bat. This winged creature was a straight up mutant killer who probably had a protein shake and Arnold Schwarzenegger for breakfast. Black as night with long, spindly legs, it also had a bulbous head with razor sharp teeth and crazy arm-like wings that could put commercial airlines out of business. The catch phrase across the photo read: Giant bat … Fuck that, I know a demon when I see one.

I laughed in measured machine gun bursts for several minutes. I still didn't have the foggiest idea why a demon bat made me laugh so hard. Perhaps it was because I imagined someone's hubby in his fugly Christmas sweater hanging from clawed talons as it flapped away into the night. Or maybe I imagined Batman getting bitch-slapped by this beast in a winner-takes-all fight for the Batcave.

Either way, it was positive to be warmed by the spread of unexpected humour. I wasted at least another hour on pointless social pursuits. In that moment, thoughts of the last few days were carefully placed under lock and key, lost to the mindlessness of internet posts.

A little after five, I received a text from *The Mother*.

It was the start of operation: check on the daughter, though it would never be admitted. Both parents planned to come over to cheer me up and remove any dangerous weapons from the apartment. *The Mother* promised no talk or long-suffering questions about *The Ex-Squeeze* and I prayed she meant it. I suspected the impromptu visit was more about assessing my mental health.

Despite perceived intentions and knowing I'd be watched, I secretly needed them. I needed them to act normal, shower me with affection and then go home, pretending all was well even if it was a horrible lie.

Their visit reaped the most incredible reward.

Joy.

Yes, I'd soiled my panties over a giant bat, but it was nothing compared to the sunset walk along the beach while spotting dolphins. Never in a million years did I expect to see such magnificent creatures frolicking in the ocean near my home. How strange that they appeared on this day of all days, right when I needed to witness perfection at an imperfect time; their innocent pursuit of happiness proved an indescribable assault on the senses.

It was a moment I'd never forget. I was lost and temporarily forgot about all inner pain. I remembered everything that was good, wholesome and real.

Day Seventeen

*H*ave you ever listened to a conversation half-heartedly; the words slurred and incoherent because of your lack of interest? Suddenly, you're fully immersed by unexpected words like 'bum rash' and 'moist'. What then?

Lunch was upon me; a welcomed reprieve from the working day. I sat prone in *The Boss's* chair, eating a tasteless lentil wrap I consumed out of habit rather than hunger. Bland paste masticated between teeth I'd neglected to brush that morning, my mind focused on thoughts of hazardous walks into the street. What would happen if I let a bus mow me down? Would I make pretty blood splatter? Would Windex really clean me off the windscreen?

You'd be amazed by the dark processes I regularly generated. I pictured innards on the sidewalk and brain matter clinging to a side mirror. I saw my face as a shredded mess and my limp body thrown several meters into the air and speared to a lamp post. How cool would that have sounded in a coroner's report?

But I digress ...

The unexpected conversation occurred while I was eating half-chewed legumes and picturing my impending death. *The Bestie* and her pregnant cousin—*The Baby Mama*—were discussing matters pertaining to *The Baby Mama's* impending birth. During talk of delivery expectancies and caesarean scars, I heard something about vaginal tearing and fruit salad.

Vaginas and Vitamin C? My ears twitched like I was Samantha

from Bewitched. I was yanked from the land of death and dismemberment and quickly waded into the mysterious and unknown world of cervical mishaps. I wasn't curious about pregnancy or the various stages of delivery, but interested in the before and after analogies jokingly passed around.

'Sex is the pleasurable stage of baby making, essentially an interlude with a lady finger banana, but then this fruit union yields a melon which grows inside and eventually begs release when ripe. All of a sudden, you have a giant pineapple attempting to seek the sun, rearing its head, spiky end first'.

I thought the spiel delivered by another colleague was poetry in motion. *The Baby Mama* wiped away a sheen of sweat, swallowed back bile and emphatically denied the entire process. I couldn't stop laughing, but I also wasn't four months pregnant with a pineapple or considering breast pumps as a lay-by option.

It occurred to me that given my interest in trivial laughter that I might be slowly losing grasp on substantial and worthy forms of intellectual conversation. Lately I seemed inspired only by talk of sex, men, sex, my giant boobs, sex or how fucking hot Zac Efron was. I skimmed over politics, religion and geography on occasion, but it didn't hold me captive. I'd always been well-rounded and interested in a variety of topics. I wondered if I'd become a developing deviant or was steadily wasting brain cells with talk of lady parts and sexual tidings.

Hmm.

The rest of the day was spent laughing at menial topics including *The Bestie* and her gas issues. She made a habit of leaving rather large deposits at the front counter and then hastily departing. I was left as the bearer of bad news for multiple clients; their judgemental and somewhat weepy eyes upon me. As each methane bomb was dropped, *The Bestie* laughed and bolted, leaving me to deal with a waiting room full of holocaust victims.

I threatened to throw a match in her direction and she stopped trying to kill us all.

I vacated the Gas Exchange a little after five and headed home to an empty apartment and long weekend alone. It was a very long week. *The Boss* was away and to be truthful, I was looking forward to her coming back and taking responsibility for the burned down staff room. I also wanted to get rip-roaring drunk, fall into a coma, deny reality and not worry about opening the doors to my shithole job on Tuesday.

I collapsed into a chair in the sunroom shortly after. I remember gazing out the window and upon the horizon. The breeze tickled my skin and I gave myself over to the semblance of peace I found until I'd sat long enough to remember everything.

I then opened a bottle of tequila and fell into that long awaited coma.

Day Eighteen

*T*oday was a good Friday—literally and emotionally. I woke up early to exercise for therapy, endorphins and the excess kilojoule burn. The session was productive.

The Bestie came over a little after nine to cheer me up. I thought she'd have been sick of me after spending all week at work with a mopey bitch and then drunken hours via phone the previous night. She wanted to apologise for trying to kill me with her anal gas and I was happy to see her regardless. Fun was on the agenda. I planned to send hate mail to celebrities with comb-overs and afros and she planned on investing time reigniting her passion for photography. Encouraging the photography thing was straightforward, but *The Bestie* insisted I leave Donald Trump and Bruno Mars alone.

We headed to the beach in search of pleasant exposure angles and tanning options; not a task easily accomplished over a long weekend. Frolicking in the ocean was better than staying indoors. I personally prayed that kids would rather play on their IPads or piss their parents off with re-runs of The Wiggles, but we weren't that lucky.

A nudist beach ensured there was no chance of invasion by minors, but it did come with a wrinkly old man with saggy balls and a tiny pecker. How I managed to control myself I'll never know.

<Insert sarcasm here>

Voyeurism aside, *The Bestie* and I focused on our tans and talked about relationship woes and stayed positive about life and matters of the heart. The company was resplendent and when teamed with laughter and cold ones from the chiller box, it was the perfect way to spend Good Friday.

What happened next? The incident is now best tailored to folklore. Honestly, it was the funniest damn thing I've ever witnessed and I'd not laughed that hard in ages.

'I have to go to the toilet,' *The Bestie* had said to me, eyes wide and full of fear.

I actually gathered this might have been the case since she'd been farting on and off for several minutes. 'Um, good luck with that,' I'd joked, knowing there was no plumbing in the general vicinity.

Her saucer eyes didn't diminish in size; her panic seemed to grow.

In most instances, copping a squat behind a bush would be the most common solution. Not *The Bestie*. She decided that the best way to pinch off a loaf was to fight with fish and the battering waves of the ocean. She clean forgot that there was this thing called social etiquette. She whipped off her bathing suit, stumbled around on the rocky bottom before smiling triumphantly at dropping her log into the deep blue beyond.

Yep. *The Bestie* shit in the ocean.

I owed her a massive thank you; not because she was comfortable enough to fertilise the great outdoors while I looked on, but because in that moment I didn't feel like the most ridiculous person in the world for holding onto wasted feelings for a man I really needed to forget and fast.

Perhaps there was a lesson to be learned. Just like *The Bestie* let go of her proverbial shit, I had to let go of mine, too. After all, if *The Ex Squeeze* had truly wanted me, he'd still be with me, wouldn't he?

Day Nineteen

*I*n recent months, Saturday had been a day ear-marked for the exploration of new terrain; whisking off to the beach, tasting new foods, hiking unexplored foothills or immersing oneself in romantic endeavours with *The Ex Squeeze*. I'd come to fear that Saturday might now be forever known as laundry and floor mopping day.

My life had been reduced to wasteful moments spent dancing with disinfectant and wiping out the oven. I'd barely cooked of late which made most of my spring cleaning redundant. I should have been tangoing at sunset with a hot Latino, sipping cocktails with cute bartenders or shoe shopping with non-existent funds. Instead I was surrounded by drying sheets, damp flooring and the distinct smell of citrus.

Don't get me wrong, being clean was good; just not how I imagined spending my free time. My social calendar was flailing, buried under a mountain of regret and longing for excitement. I decided that I needed to go burn some energy before the urge to re-thread the timber blinds overcame me.

I jumped in the car and headed to a hiking trail near town; previous experience had shown that I usually finished within an hour and a half—a most excellent workout session, but also risky since it was known for its dangerous terrain. Hiking there had not boded well for me during past jaunts. I'd fractured my ankle after dancing with a jutting rock and then had rolled several meters down a cliff face. I'd been chased by a pissed off goanna who hadn't appreciated my photography skills. I'd been a heartbeat away from standing on a suspect snake while debating the meaning of life and also embarrassed myself horribly by belting out tunes at an approaching hiker I somehow did not see.

Today was no exception to my uncanny ability to make an ass of myself.

The cyclone had littered the trail with fallen trees, rocks and in this instance, wait-a-while; think of vines with hundreds of razor blades vying to take up residence in your flesh and make you scream for pleasure.

Well, I kicked an entire thatch of wait-a-while right into the back of my own ankle. I bled uncontrollably and screamed at the top of my lungs. Seventeen horns hooked into my flesh and I expelled seventeen equally impressive expletives to match. I had no water, no phone, no bandages and was only half way around the trail. Shit like that only ever happened to me. Add a freak rainstorm while slowly bleeding out and my day and mood were well and truly made! It would be safer playing chicken on the damn highway!

By the time I reached the car I congratulated myself on my restraint. I avoided kicking several hikers in the crotch after pointing out my very obvious gaping wound. Gee, thanks. I never would have fucking noticed all the blood gushing from my leg!

Deep breaths.

A lot of other stuff happened in the following few hours, but I couldn't recall most of it. I chose to block the bad experience regarding an impromptu meet with *The Ex Squeeze* or maybe I was actually contracted by the government to eradicate toads by way of wooden baton. Running through people's backyards whacking the crap out of pests was the excuse I was inclined to want to believe at the time.

After my amphibious undertaking, I headed to *The Bestie's* house to alter my negative attitude and explore more entertaining options for the evening rather than continued wallowing. I still hadn't shed tears, but it was steadily getting on top of me, threatening to take over and crumble the hastily constructed walls I'd built since …

The Bestie and *The Baby Mama* and I went out for an insanely large dinner I avoided spewing up later followed by a few games of pool and copious amounts of cider. My pant zipper exploded with my food baby, but being out with friends helped stem the pain. I still felt emotionally slain, but also wasn't the only woman on the planet to feel like this. I was one among a mass of many mopey, single ladies searching for that little slither of lasting happiness.

I guess I just wondered if I'd ever find it and successfully hold onto it.

Day Twenty

*S*unday … the day for rest; funny how I really didn't need it. I was tired after yesterday's impromptu meeting with the Ex, but chose not to keep lingering on it. Besides, I couldn't rest even if I wanted to; being alone was a silent killer.

The apartment was scrubbed clean. I couldn't bleach and disinfect anymore. I needed to occupy myself. I figured that watching DVD's was the best form of mindless, lack-lustre entertainment.

I even attempted to write for a while. Words weren't usually an issue for me. If I couldn't find scintillating ones, then I could muster abusive ones to add to whatever story I decided to craft. I just needed to keep busy—just needed to avoid being entirely unamused, alone and crumbling under the weight of my own vicious thoughts.

How could I shake this funk? I was so sick of myself and my dour mood swings that I considered head-butting a wall for peace. More than anything, I wanted the happiness I'd sought at the beginning of the journey, but instead of being happy, I'd started to get angry. Why? Because I'd started to believe that perhaps happiness might hinge on the returned affections of a man.

I was a strong, independent woman who refused to shed tears and yet I was weakened by this notion of need. Why couldn't I switch my brain off for a few weeks and get on with the business of living and having fun again? Why couldn't I reject cynicism, self-doubt and find peace in the unknown? That ridiculously inquisitive part of myself wondered if Mary really had a little lamb or Bear Grilles really enjoyed the taste of his own urine. I needed to know why I wasn't good enough to love or why I wasn't first choice, but that was another pointless form of torture. I'd never be able to answer those questions; everything was speculative. I had to let it go.

I dyed my hair instead and went to *The Family's* house to indulge home-cooked tucker, get fat and watch B grade movies about pornographic robots. We watched other horror films that scared the beejesus out of me and talked only briefly about my woes. By eleven o'clock, I kissed everyone good night and made the arduous journey home. I wanted to stay, curl up in my parent's bed and pretend the world didn't exist, but it wasn't logical. Life would continue to move forward even while I remained stationary.

It really was time to get those legs moving. I just wished I could figure out how.

Day Twenty-One

*T*oday was the last day of the Easter weekend and with its end came creeping sadness, the kind that delayed bed because I knew I'd be right back to the daily grind within hours.

I decided to make the most of it; go to a gorge with a couple of mates and lay in the sun and swim the day away, but, like any outdoor plans made, a freak thunderstorm forced me back into boredom and indoors. I began to wonder if I might be a demigod; the half child of the goddess of cloud and rain. My presence or the mere mention that I might leave the house always seemed to incite water to fall rapidly and inconveniently from above.

A massive tantrum on the horizon, I stowed the urge to roll around and kick my legs in disgust. *The Bestie* suggested a road trip to which I quickly agreed. It also didn't hurt that we stuffed half the supermarket confectionary aisle into the car while we blasted our tender ear drums with epic tunes from the stereo.

We headed north, treading familiar ground that encouraged thoughts of recent weekends spent dangling from the tree canopy nearby, but I decided the company coveted in the present was better than the past. We went on to enjoy a mediocre lunch at an outdoor café where I paid far too much for Barramundi and *The Bestie* was hungry again an hour later.

The village offered little in the way of entertainment and we were rolling back home again an hour later. It didn't matter because we weren't sightseeing. We were filling in time and creating distractions.

On the way back, *The Bestie* and I stopped to roll a seriously injured hitchhiker off the road and into the bushes. An accident. I hadn't hit him that hard and he'd seriously come out of nowhere!

The next stop was a sleepy seaside town; we thought we should tell someone that a Lithuanian backpacker might be dying about ten miles back; *The Bestie* was also inspired to take happy snaps of the surrounding landscape.

The local authorities thanked us for keeping the highways clean and told us not to worry about the hit and run incident. Hitchhiking was illegal and the Lithuanian had it coming. This seemed mildly disturbing, but we shrugged and went about our business.

So we continued on to pursue *The Bestie's* interest in photography. Rather like my flailing writing career, she was having trouble reconnecting with her creative side. Finding that spark within was complicated; just as I thought mine was forever buried with a part of my soul I'd left in a distant past.

As I watched her click away, I found a sense of peace. It was okay that I was dragging my feet and struggled to get my life back on track. I figured I needed time to heal—to find myself again and to remember that the past, the people and the places that once brought me joy would eventually come back if I allowed it.

I may not ever become a successful writer, but at least I'd found words again. I could only hope that this reawakening would continue to inspire others like *The Bestie* to invest in her passion, even if it seemed insurmountable and pointless. Passions should never be suppressed or allowed to perish no matter how hard we may try to stifle its naturally flourishing nature.

Day Twenty-Two

*F*irst day back at work and it wasn't as bad as I thought with *The Boss* still away. It might have been the pep-talk I'd had with myself at 5.00am.

The alarm sounded like any other morning; a ridiculous tune to refresh me from sleep, when in reality, it scared the absolute shit out of me. I fell out of bed, rubbed sleep-laden eyes and grunted all the way to the bathroom. I exercised (not in the bathroom), showered and made it to work before the sun poked its beaming smile above the horizon.

I sat at *The Boss's* desk, quiet for several minutes, pleased that I still had at least an hour of solitude before other staff arrived. I thought about writing, starting payroll or mulling over data entry, but I didn't do any of that. I sat there, thinking about the word that floated through my mind at 5.00am.

Acceptance.

I had to congratulate myself on completing a twelve step program in as little as a week. I didn't remember the denial or anger stage, but I suppose that could have been the Tequila. It'd been that long since *The Ex Squeeze* had offered friendship and other misguided forms of bullshit and for that entire week I'd moped, wondered and waited for some sort of sign that perhaps my affections had not been entirely wasted since we'd begun dating.

Wasted time was an integral part of fallen relationships despite the lessons learned and the memories gleaned. The trick was knowing when to accept finality. I had no more control over *The Ex Squeeze's* actions, thoughts or feelings than I had my own. Waiting for him to come to his senses or for me to rediscover my effervescence was completely and utterly insane!

Don't get me wrong. My chest ached for him, but he wasn't my entire world. I had wonderful friends, a beautiful family and if I was truthful, plenty going for me. I didn't need him or anyone to bring purpose to my life.

I could no longer obsess over a situation I had zero control. *The Ex Squeeze* had made choices and I'd made mine. I'd put my faith in fate's hands, trusted that she knew what she was doing and that this last week of unknowns and tumultuous pain had purpose—all of it leading somewhere sublime. Thus my acceptance of the situation was born and my sadness ebbed. For the first time in 168hrs, I started to see clearly and think rationally.

Everything would be alright …

I smiled at work today, knowing it was the start of another new chapter in my life. I intended to go back to planning for adventure, intrigue and hopefully a little bit of romance. I'd make good choices and even reconciled that my body needed to be healthy not just outside, but in. My spirit soared with this revelation—and with it—darkness grasped by the scruff of its neck and cast out into the light.

I remember being excited for what was yet to come …

Day Twenty-Three

I'd like to say that something absolutely fabulous happened to me today, but it would be a horrid lie. I suppose I could count jumping into a chalk painting, dancing with penguins and horse racing on a merry-go-round. Did I mention my awesome shoes that matched my umbrella; the tool I used to fend off these weird characters that sang 'Supercalifragilistic-something' at me?

Alas, it was an ordinary Wednesday, another working day and I had absolutely nothing new to report. I accepted my current circumstances and still hadn't shed tears, but also knew I wasn't completely alright, especially if I believed I was hanging with Mary Poppins.

Tall tales aside, I was supposed to be searching or even stumbling upon one hundred days of happiness. I was disappointed that my joyous occasion for the day hinged on eating pickles from the jar for dinner.

Eating the lazy out-of-jar dish proved I needed to take time to invest in me for a while and figure out what makes me happy outside the world of romantic interludes. I needed to be okay being by myself, accomplish tasks without social media recognition and attempt the ultimate … falling in love with *me* again.

Day Twenty-Four

I engaged drastic measures this morning and checked out of social media for the foreseeable future. I was no longer drawn to the notification lights flashing on my phone or hoping to receive shallow validation through the 'likes' and 'comments' of those I'd hastily friended over the internet. I ignored lewd posts and insanely funny pictures, all in an attempt to avoid being slammed with reminders of my lingering unhappiness.

I decided that working on being alone and being content in my own company was infinitely more important than keeping socially informed. I'd been with someone in one way or another for over sixteen years and realised that despite enjoying my solitude on most occasions, being entirely by myself was somewhat of a struggle.

These days I found myself easily bored, distracted and relentlessly in pursuit of the next action-packed activity. Sitting silently and still was a marvellous challenge I had no real desire to complete, but since it had become clear that my urges moved in the direction of requiring the steely embrace of a lover to be happy, I decided I needed to be bitch-slapped into some semblance of order.

So on this day, twenty-four days into the one hundred day journey, I noted it as an obstacle both challenging and requiring resolution. I needed to discover myself, work on the joy in solitude and hopefully stumble upon the inner peace and happiness I so desperately sought.

Day Twenty-Five

*A*nzac Day. I was disgraced to say that this momentous occasion for diggers all across my great nation meant little more to me than the official proclamation that I was a quarter way through my one hundred days towards happiness.

I should be shot or punched in the tits—preferably the latter since I was certain I'd recover. Thousands of men had given their lives for a cause so much greater than my own and yet I'd spent at least half of my journey feeling sad and sorry for myself.

Yeah, I needed a swift kick to the vagina while someone was at it. I needed to stop whingeing and get my mojo back. There were only seventy-five days remaining and more than anything, I needed to get my act together. I wanted an off the charts, crazy sexual experience, travel to a foreign destination and then shave someone's eyebrows off for a belly laugh. There were some other, more important goals to try to achieve, too, but I had to start somewhere.

I started by cleaning the car; seriously uninteresting and didn't involve soapy sex on the hood, but a necessity after the hit and run. There was gooey skin debris in my grill-work that had started to attract flies. I also vacuumed up a family of hairballs, evicted a few spiders and sniffed old Chinese takeout containers for edible possibilities.

Don't judge me.

After that thrilling chore, I headed to *The Bestie's* house for coffee and a chat. In some small measure I expected her to amuse me and I quickly realised I was circling the dependency drain. What I needed to do was leave her alone to focus on her own self-growth and for me to concentrate on mine.

I started said journey by watching a small mountain of DVD's; ordinary to most, but since I'd left my husband, pastimes I used to enjoy had become insanely mundane. I had no focus or urge to be still and calm without feeling compelled to break the monotony with social interaction of any variety.

I'll admit I struggled to watch the small pile of motion pictures, so I moved onto something else I used to enjoy in the hopes that perhaps I'd still appreciate the activity—reading. Sounded simple enough, but the longest thing I'd read in over a year was my grocery list. I think in the end I might have read the TV Guide.

I went to bed that night a little before midnight. I'd been alone for over twelve hours and had not uttered a single word. I watched three movies, one episode of a TV show, become knowledgeable with free-to-air programing for the week and fell asleep with a romance novel in-hand. The spine on said novel remained uncracked, but I suppose it was the thought that really counted.

Day Twenty-Six
to
Day Forty-Seven

Blaaahhhh …
.

Day Forty-Eight

*E*verything had gone to shit over the last twenty odd days; my inner calm, my masterful plan to hold back tears, the decision to remain positive though truly believing the world was crumbling around me—it had been all for naught.

I'd unravelled like a piece of old twine and lost control of my emotional self. I'd been like a dormant volcano, quietly fuelling an explosion to break the crust's surface and spew molten pain in every direction. I could no longer contain every ounce of inner turmoil, anger or fear I'd bottled.

I'd even stopped writing. I'd stopped smiling and thinking rationally. I'd shut down, my heart compromised and no longer capable of dealing with what I ultimately deemed rejection. I couldn't talk about it and I couldn't stop extremes between tears and laughter—most of all—I hadn't wanted to subject anyone reading this to a further twenty days of woe-is-fucking-me.

So I didn'tt.

Today I came back to reality, came up for air and looked around at the world with renewed eyes. I knew—after much internal dialogue—that I'd started to fall in love as quickly as I'd run from it. The hardest part was knowing I'd played a part in the demise of my own happiness, despite certain complications that would have undoubtedly unfolded within the relationship.

On this day—forty-eight days into the journey—I could finally admit that I was okay. I stopped allowing my mind to wander towards errant thoughts of an unchangeable past or hoping for a future that no longer belonged to me. I accepted that happiness couldn't be found solely in the embrace of the opposite sex and their ever-changing perceptions of me. It could only be found in the desire to accept the things I cannot change and to embrace all that I'd been and would be.

How did I get over this little bump in the road? How did I wash *The Ex Squeeze* right out of my hair and move forward despite the ache in my heart?

I started sleeping with extremely hot men.

I did a whole bunch of other self-discovery stuff, too, but that seemed vaguely boring in comparison. I'd had an extremely sexy military man who knew exactly how to push my buttons, a Greek fireman who spent hours putting out flames with his tongue and a whole host of other buff and multilingual men who were *still* happy to make me *happy*.

Stop shaking your heads at me!

I also spent a great deal of time alone, analysing who I was and who I want to be. I felt confident that emotional breakdowns no longer lurked behind my heart valves or stumbled through my brainwaves. I'd thought long and hard about many things— especially before my knickers started flying free and strange men vied to make my bed springs groan.

Of course, many saw fit to offer opinion on my recent behaviour, branding my situation 'less than ideal' as I apparently had not allowed sufficient time to heal, but I'd never been very patient. I had no inclination to rehash the past; thus, the Band-Aid of distraction had worked masterfully. I'd laughed hard, orgasmed regularly and started to live with reckless abandon—the kind that made the tightly-coiled envious. I was freer than I'd ever been and happier than I expected or believed I could be. I looked forward to the future and it had nothing to do with sex and everything to do with the confidence and self-understanding I'd developed.

Truthfully, I was curious to see what the next fifty days would bring.

Day Forty-Nine

*G*lorious righteousness; it's not often I can say that, but today I knew it to be true—especially now that I'd returned to singing in the car at the top of my lungs, eating ridiculous amounts of junk food and getting out regularly. I smiled unabashedly at attractive men, wiggled my hips like Shakira and generally felt great about being alive, single, and positive.

Today was Monday and I was uber-refreshed after a jam-packed weekend. I felt ready to take on the world head-on and hence, ploughed through work like I was a farmer on crack; smiling, laughing and generally inviting a good time to be had by all. Complaints were non-existent and productivity high.

It wasn't the same with *The Bestie* away on holidays. Usually there'd be mischief to manage, but since she'd been gone, mischief had become a concept rather than an actualisation.

People often described us as trouble, though I decided not to count the hit and run, ocean defecation, staffroom arson or buried bodies as mischief. Work may have been rather ordinary without her, but I survived. In fact, I was heading home before I realised, on a mission to clean up and poof my hair for the first table service date I'd accepted since *The Ex Squeeze* and I had parted ways.

Sure, I'd been busy rubbing up against some very sexy, very emotionally unavailable men, but this was different. The gentleman who'd captured my attention had scintillating phone skills and a cheeky smile; his Irish accent didn't hurt either or his apparent need to chase.

I liked being chased.

Metaphorically.

Not actually chased, like with a butcher's knife and a ski mask. That shit's uncalled for.

Anyway, I think from memory I looked pretty fabulous in my little black and white number with red heels. My hair was doing exactly what it had been told and my make-up didn't make headway for every crevice in my thirty-something-year-old face.

During self-admiration, my phone flashed; the green orb of unpredictable content. I momentarily wondered if perhaps *The Irishman* (this was what I'd started calling him) might have cancelled. That would have been super annoying after spending an hour getting ready, but it was *The Cockney*.

I hadn't heard from him for a few weeks; not his fault since I'd ignored quite a few of his recent messages in lieu of my depressed state. Strange that he contacted me now on this night of all nights!

'Hi, how are you?' he'd said.

I quickly typed back, 'I'm actually doing really well. I'm sorry I haven't text you much lately, lots happening.'

'No problem, everyone gets busy.'

'Thanks,' was my lacklustre response. I noticed that he was writing in return, but I didn't have the time to wait for his message. I was running behind for my first date with *The Irishman* and didn't want to miss the entree.

I decided that since this was the first date, I needed an escape plan—namely my own vehicle. *The Irishman* may have crusty boogar build-up in his nose or ridiculously long fingernails caked with dirt. Psychopathic killer was also a classic option, but if freaky shit of any kind went down, I would make a mad dash for the exit and tear up the highway home.

He wasn't what I expected or even what I was used to. There were no introductory compliments, lingering looks of appreciation during the meal or immediate plans for a secondary date. He didn't touch me and didn't share his dessert which was a massive strike against him. I was left befuddled. The conversation was excellent and our interaction on the whole both entertaining and comfortable, but where was the spark?

A part of me expected a bundle of interchangeable nerves to drift across the starched white linens between us, his fingers accidentally grazing mine as we reached for the cutlery. Perhaps I read far too many romance novels or maybe I hoped for something more than ordinary—and honestly—why shouldn't I yearn for something spectacularly different, complex and passionate?

I didn't even receive a goodnight kiss.

It was probable—based on quick assumption—I was either on a first date with Mr Boring and Uptight or the last remaining gentleman on the planet. I still wasn't sure whether to be intrigued or downright disappointed. At least the food had been excellent.

By the time I arrived home, I was knackered. Being intellectually scintillating was exhausting and my face ached from forced smiles.

Before turning in, I quickly checked my phone as always; that taunting green light flashed in the top left corner.

The Cockney. I'd forgotten about him. I finally took the time to read his message, the one I couldn't be bothered waiting for earlier.

'I know it's short notice, but I was wondering if you'd like to meet up for coffee tonight?'

Day Fifty

*I*t was the half way mark and I'd spent at least a quarter of it moping and feeling sorry for myself. Was it okay to call myself a massive loser?

Life had begun again and it was definitely time to start living it! I refused to spend the next fifty days feeling anything other than excitement, joy, wonder and hope. If I couldn't get my act together at any particular point, then I had decided to inspire happiness in someone else; a beautiful sentiment.

Today was a good day. I made money and ate so as not to perish; great day, end of story. Kidding.

I clocked on at work, lined my purse with a few extra dollars, but also drifted through the day without concern for the past few weeks, smiled with ease and general contentment. I ignored bikini shots on social media posted by *The Ex Squeeze* of someone he was currently bedding. She had fugly teeth and an ass you could park a bike between. Who was really winning?

After work, I took my customary walk along the esplanade to help alleviate any building concerns and flush me with endorphins. My mind wandered to *The Bestie* who usually accompanied me on such walks; I missed her little button face. She still had two weeks of holiday remaining, so I had no choice but to soldier on without her calming presence and rational thought process.

A poor substitute, I then met with another acquaintance for sushi after my walk. This acquaintance would remain forever nameless, mostly because she was like the extra on my movie set, the token knob-head that said things like: dang girl, that's whack and uh huh, you know it, girlfriend.

Do you know the kind I'm talking about? She was the one who never gave a shit about me, but always filled time with trivial laughter, her racist point-of-view and grossly inappropriate conversations.

Anyway, we talked shite and laughed over rice. She judged my current sexual promiscuity and I laughed about her endless quest for the perfect body, despite her belief that owning a gym membership trumped the results of actual attendance.

It seemed silly to admit that I missed nights like these when of late my life was an ongoing foray into dinner, drinks and dates. I think what I mean is that I missed simple social interaction and was enjoying it now. I dissolved a good, honest marriage to explore this terrain so it was imperative to embrace it and try to remember and appreciate not just the people in my life, but the absolute freedom I'd acquired since my divorce to be able to accept dinner invites from potty-mouthed friends while munching on raw fish.

Day Fifty-One

A fever had taken hold of my usually healthy and able body today. I was ice cold, but subjected to a head swathed in intolerable heat that rhythmically pounded without respite. My nose was congested and my eyes were blurred.

I stayed at work as long as I could because bills needed to be paid and I never wanted to earn the title of freaking pussy, but I was sent home around three-thirty, dropping my belongings all over the apartment as I arrived. Clothes were torn from my body and strewn across the floor. I collapsed onto my bed seconds later, eyes closing and my body giving up. For too long I'd allowed my vagina to dictate my sleeping patterns and thus, had spent far too many nights ignoring the call of rest which I desperately needed.

I passed out for two blissful hours and unaware of reality when I was rudely awakened by a text message from *The Irishman*. He suggested another meet-up that night and honestly, despite my pounding head and fluctuating body temperature, my lady parts started to scream at me; seriously, tiny little voices echoed within my cervix that told me to get out of bed, shower and get some loving.

Common sense dictated that I should stay home, relax and acquire more sleep, but I was starting to fear that I was absent of logic. I foolishly followed my chatty vagina's advice and agreed to meet. This time I suggested a coffee at my place, mostly because I hoped for a little slap and tickle on the sofa and partly because I wasn't sure I'd make it into town without vomiting.

The Irishman appeared on my doorstep within the hour. We sat upon my sofa, laughed and discussed life, but the excitement ended there. We didn't hold hands, he didn't kiss me and his eyes were more than appropriately at eye level the entire time we conversed. I began to wonder about this guy. Did he bat for the other team? Had he recently undergone penile surgery? Did I have a giant boogar on my face? Could he hear my vagina?

Apparently I'd begun to date a new breed of man—a man I was uncertain I liked. More to the point, I was unsure about actually dating someone again so soon. The truth was that it was easier slipping and sliding between bed sheets than developing an actual relationship that could lead to feelings again.

Feelings.

They were the ultimate dirty word at this point.

Day Fifty-Two

What can be said when the day was filled with talk of all things decidedly erotic? Should I have denied my involvement, pretended that for an hour I hadn't giggled over sagging balls and extra-large foreskin? Should I have berated my filthy mind when surrounded by other, like-minded, bored, overly-sexed females?

I can't lie; once a deviant always a deviant.

A month ago I was in a relationship, languid in the embrace of a satisfying and ultimately normal sex life. I'd since been living the dream of all promiscuous men, swimming in a sea of varying semen and now laughed about the antics with friends. My lunch talk was now based on experience, no longer the subjective.

Thirsty Thursday gathered new momentum; no longer an ode to the after work drink, but rather, the rush to go home to a friend, lover or husband and show them just how parched forthright women were. I was no longer concerned about the judgement of others, but rather, pleased to see my mojo return.

Today I made several girls clutch their stomachs as riotous snorts of laughter took hold. Tears and gasping breath left every mouth, the stories of my recent exploits tossed about like old fables at a campfire. It was surprising to learn how truly filthy all of us were.

I'm ashamed in some ways to admit that this was my happy moment for the day. I helped clients, achieved control over outstanding work, but it was nothing compared to an hour of nonsensical amusement. The wildly inappropriate work conversation stretched a smile almost a mile wide across my face and coincidentally cheered up those not as proactive as I was in my attempts to achieve happiness. Sombre moods lifted and a carefree attitude was adopted by all for the rest of the afternoon. If nothing else, that was a massive accomplishment.

Who knew blow jobs and kinky sex could incite such results?

Day Fifty-Three

*H*appy Friday one and all; my favourite day of the week; more so today since *The Boss* let me have an early mark! At 2.00pm I threw my bag over my shoulder and headed out. My mission was to get in a quick jog before heading home to do a bit of much needed editing on a previously collated novel. I wasn't sure I'd be successful given my recent track record, but I planned to have a stab at it anyway.

The sun shone brightly in the late afternoon sky, serving only to exacerbate my sweat fest. Ordinarily I would be ecstatic, but today I couldn't get my rhythm and the intense UV rays paired with uncoordinated jogging became a bad joke. My four kilogram weight gain since the break-up made more difference than I wanted to believe. I was sweating and sucking down oxygen like an emphysema patient!

I finished up moments before impending death and quickly headed to a local coffee shop to dose up on caffeine. I had the very best of intentions to order a water and salad, but exited with a large chai latte and a blueberry muffin—a sucker for sweets.

While I woofed down the sugary delights, I had a brief communication with *The Irishman*. We discussed plans for our upcoming date. Ideas of romantic interludes on the beach with wine and peanut butter were on track for ruin since the forecasted weather wasn't brilliant. More rain? Seriously? If I could shove an umbrella up someone's orifice to instigate some sort of permanent atmospheric change, I absolutely would.

Mid complaint, I looked down at my vibrating phone to see *The Cockney's* message icon blinking. I realised that I hadn't responded to his coffee invite. In fact, I'd taken one look at the message, screwed my face up in confusion and ignored the perfectly reasonable offer. It was the first time in a long time I had no idea what to say or what to do; his genuine nature befuddled me!

I'd had no problem of late getting cosy with new men, but *The Cockney* was in a league of his own—the kind of league where I was unsure if I wanted to join or if I believed I was inadequate. I didn't think he was too good for me, I'd just labelled him special. And, while dicking around, I didn't want to screw up potential perfection with constant indecision.

Perhaps a sixth sense existed within. Not the kind that identified dead people under my mattress or those parading up and down the corridor at midnight, but the intuition to understand how a person, a moment or a memory could hold a flame within. *The Cockney* could ultimately bring me the happiness I sought. I suspect that's why I pushed my 'potential flame' aside, worried I'd somehow douse its vibrancy before it had a chance to burn.

Like anything, I figured I'd know or be given a sign when the timing was one hundred percent right. For now—life as per usual without drama.

I remember not having any complaints about the day or noteworthy moments of joy that required written celebration. I was just content. Work ended early, exercise concluded—despite the sweaty stench that still clung to my skin—the tunes pumped and curling up on the sofa with coffee and zero plans of commitment seemed like a pretty sweet way to end the week.

Day Fifty-Four

Where to start; there were so many happy moments to celebrate today I didn't have enough words to express every detail with perfect clarity. First, it was Saturday, my favourite day of the week and it began rather early. I'd had a rubbish night's sleep littered with thoughts of *The Ex-Squeeze* test-driving every bronzed brunette in the city, but I had to shake it off; an awesome day trip with *The Family* was planned.

It was the perfect day to hunt through bric-a-brac at the markets and enjoy the first batch of consistent sun seen in weeks. It didn't matter that the market were sheltered by weeping willows that smothered me with icy shadow. It didn't matter that the ground was a slush fest and I'd forgotten my jumper; piping hot coffees and fresh fudge kept us warm.

We consumed enough caffeine that our jittery selves sat surprisingly content while eating lunch at a high-priced café with poor service and ridiculously small portion sizes. It also didn't matter that we remained hungry because *The Father* smuggled bags of homemade chocolate under his shirt which we happily consumed in the car on the way home. *The Mother* attempted to lecture him about five finger discounts, but since it was around a mouthful of creamy, indulgent dark chocolate, her argument faded.

I returned to the apartment a little after 2.00pm and was sad to see *The Family* drive away, but since I had a million text messages waiting for me—most of them from eager men or friends curious of my evening plans—I decided not to dwell.

The first message was from *The Cockney*. I was surprised to hear from him. I thought that by ignoring his invitation that he might give up on me, but there was his message, flashing in the corner of my screen, completely underserving.

'Hi,' he'd said. 'I haven't heard from you. I hope you're okay. I have to go out of town for a few weeks for work. Hopefully we can catch up when I come back ...'

What was with this man? After several months of talking and messaging, he'd finally invited me for coffee only to be rebuked by my ignorance. How could he still be interested in conversing with someone too rude to respond to an innocent caffeinated tryst?

The simplest answer was that he was ...

I quickly responded with a picture of a 'thumbs up'. Yup, I sent a wordless gesture because I was lame and had no idea what else to say, what to promise or even how to apologise for my poor behaviour. If he ever messaged me again I'd have been truly surprised. I was an idiot and he was ... yeah ...

Anyway, I scrolled through the next batch of messages and was left with a lot of new, non-permanent options in the male department. *The Irishman* asked to see me, so he took precedent; a romantic walk on the beach followed by dinner and who knew what was as good a place as any to start.

I wasn't excited, but I was looking forward to a nice meal and good company. *The Irishman* was a pleasant man. He had gorgeous green eyes and particularly nice fingernails that I imagined were cleaned with a toothpick while sitting in his tidy-whities on the edge of a roll top bathtub. I had no idea why my imagination ran rampant in such ways, but it kept the dating scene interesting.

We agreed to meet at five. I wore a white summer dress and was secretly pleased when those luminous eyes roamed the length of me appreciatively. His smile allured and his laugh was filled with warmth, but I was disappointed that being with him didn't invoke anything particularly inspiring within. I waited for a field's worth of butterflies to unleash themselves within my digestive tract, but alas, tumbleweeds stroked my innards with emptiness.

We laid for hours on an old, tartan blanket on the beach, talking and actively avoiding all physical contact. Conversation flowed thick and fast, but I began to wonder when he planned on taking serious advantage of me. I introduced him to the wonders of a peanut butter and chocolate union and hoped he'd want to apply it liberally to my freshly landscaped lady parts. Why else would I bring two fresh jars and no spoons on a date?

Hunger set in. We lapped up the nutty, chocolate goodness while minutes ticked by and ideas of rolling around naked and covered in confectionary slipped into oblivion. I had no choice but to accept that *The Irishman* was a complete dud.

We ate a light dinner at a nearby restaurant—in turn—I was eaten by the local bug populace and swallowed a fly during a mouthful of salad. I consumed three glasses of wine and plied him with beer in the hopes he'd turn into some sort of indecent booby-grabber.

Eventually we headed back to my apartment where we sat like awkward teens on my sofa, talking and staring at one another like idiots. After an hour it was clear I'd have to take matters into my own hands. I leant forward, bridged the gap between us and kissed him. I pressed tender lips in eagerness, tasting his mouth as if I were starving and after the ridiculous length of time it had taken for this moment to occur, I might be!

Was it worth the wait?

It was always strange to kiss someone for the first time; lips malleable, sweet and often independent of the mind. They move based on the raging beat of my heart, the quickness of breath and the taste of wild passion that comes to my tongue. I felt every physical result of this exciting new touch and it didn't take long for us to get lost in combined movements and fall into bed.

Hours passed. In fact, it was 2.00am before we realised how long we'd been kissing, touching and teasing. *The Irishman* had asked to stay the night and I let him, knowing I'd get to revel longer in this sensuous communion. I also hoped I could finally get him to take his pants off! So far he was adamant about keeping them on! What kind of red-blooded male engaged in foreplay with zero intent to follow through?

I considered crabs, three testicles or a possible vagina.

We never sealed the deal. He'd been insistent on waiting and I'd wanted his lacklustre ass out of my bed and venturing home, but it had been two o'clock in the morning and I was trapped in the warm embrace of an Irish virgin with a raging hard on and willpower cast from titanium.

Happy Sunday!

Day Fifty-Five

I'd had worse Sunday mornings. Today I woke up in the arms of a man who looked at me like I'd somehow hung the moon; a goofy grin was set upon his pale face as he hugged me tight and whispered all sorts of sweet nothings in my ear.

I didn't complain. I'd never get sick of hearing how gorgeous I am, how perfect my body appeared or even how cute my bed hair looked—yet despite incessant compliments—I still was at a loss as to what to do with the sexless Leprechaun. We indulged in continuous lip action until the wee hours, but my knickers were still firmly elasticised to my sweet spot.

No sex. I didn't remember taking a vow of celibacy. I had no understanding of his need to take things moronically slow.

We emerged from bed around nine, ruffled and desperately in need of satiation. We kissed and parted ways; he had a dog at home desperate for food and I had plans to punish my body with a run and that was exactly what I did. I spent two hours running a lengthy trail to expend the pent up energy, but the calorie burn was quickly negated. I ended up at *The Parent's* place, raided their fridge and tucked into *The Mother's* baked goods. I swallowed advice dished on *The Irishman*, too—a result of my tired looking eyes.

The Father—as always—kept his lips tightly sealed, mostly because he never got a word in edgewise. I could have sworn he was secretly pleased with my movements despite gallivanting around town with my skirt over-head. I was living life, something

I'd failed miserably in the past to negotiate.

After eating everything in sight, I headed home for a nap—not something I made a habit of. I often made fun of people who needed geriatric naps, but since I'd had about three hours sleep since Friday, I was running on empty. I remember face-planting the couch an hour later and not emerging until I was swimming in a puddle of my own drool.

The rest of the afternoon played out dully compared to dry-humping and market stall hunting. I watched television and then dragged my ass to bed again around ten. I was all round spectacularly content with the weekend despite being physically wasted and horny as hell. It didn't matter that trying to navigate a dud vibrator in desperate need of battery replacement turned into far too much work before bed.

I was too tired to care.

Day Fifty-Six

*T*here were one hundred different reasons not to be happy about Mondays, but today I chose to see only positives; whether that was because I had a decent weekend or was determined to be a bright spark for the rest of the week, I'd never know.

I worked diligently and helped a colleague make some tough financial decisions. I enjoyed a nice lunch from the café and ended the day with my usual walk along the esplanade. I chatted briefly with *The Irishman* and indulged a lovely long, hot shower that ended with me curled on the couch watching television.

The highlight of my day was calling *The Bestie*. We'd texted while she'd been away, but hadn't spoken. She was my Dr Phil. She'd also stab an enemy in the face with a pick axe and help me steal a car should the occasion call for it, but I settled for just hearing her voice.

The Bestie had ways of tempering my unpredictable moods and raging moronic thought processes. She reminded me often of who I was and the person I strived to become. She could instil confidence and also keep me grounded. I needed her guidance now before I hopped in the car, hunted down *The Irishman* and molested him.

We spoke for hours; rather unusual for me. I generally ran out of phone dialogue within ten minutes. I needed interaction—facial features or body language to retain interest, but since she was relaying aspects of her holiday, we had plenty of ongoing banter to fight off my boredom. She was also in a fabulously good mood, so I held back asking sex advice on account of not wanting to disrupt her carefree demeanour.

She was kicking holiday goals and gaining weight by the second. My pursuits were trivial in comparison; the point—to be able to hear the voice of someone I loved today, smash work goals and help out a friend who sucked the life out of every credit card and savings account they owned. All-in-all, it was a good start to the week.

Day Fifty-Seven

I pushed the fast-forward button and decided only to
document the end of the working day. Why? Who really gave
a shite about the paperwork I filed or the customers I
considered releasing a hive of angry bees upon. Besides, *The Baby
Mama* and I were off to dinner and a movie—far more
entertaining.

These impromptu dates would hopefully turn into a habit. We
both missed *The Bestie* terribly and found comfort in eating copious
amounts of junk food and engaging in ridiculous conversation
together.

Italian was the order of the day. I'd like to say that we walked
into a restaurant and ordered the rippling descendants of the Gods
to feed us grapes and satisfy our womanly desires, but realistically,
chicken parmigiana was the result of ordering from our very
impatient waiter. He didn't find it amusing when I asked for a side
of Leonardo Di Caprio.

The Baby Mama and I enjoyed getting plump on starchy
carbohydrates, indulging in boy talk and broaching the even scarier
topic of her impending birth. I'd never been so scared for anyone
in my life. I couldn't correlate how a watermelon squeezed out of a
pea-sized hole without blowing apart her uterus. She was a baby
herself; tender at nineteen and perhaps even less prepared for
motherhood than I was for the fallout on the scales the next day.

My stomach knotted just contemplating the buckets of blood in the delivery room. What if there was so much of it they couldn't see the baby coming and it fell onto the floor? I even wondered if babies bounced. *The Mother* said I was dropped on my head as a child. She believed that explained a lot about me.

The Baby Mama was far more mature than me. She opted not to dissect the planned birthing ritual any more than was necessary. Taking out insurance on her beloved uterus was an additional finance she could ill-afford!

After a fairly lengthy dinner, we headed to the cinemas. It was a while since I'd indulged. Like I mentioned before, I struggled to remain focused. It was odd that I even enjoyed the movie about a cheating husband and the friendship shared between the multiple mistresses and current wife. I related to all of the women on different levels while I relished ice-cream and nibbled on lollies.

It was sad to drop *The Baby Mama* home at the end of the night. Alone again, I convinced myself that a late night text to *The Irishman* was a great way to end an incredibly pleasant evening. I'd already broken rule number one—never text them first.

I held my breath and waited for the sound of his reply, but the text never came. I wanted to whip myself for such stupidity. I also went on to break rule number two—never chase! I decided to dice the phone and forget about it. Perhaps I should forget him, too?

Stupid, sexless Leprechaun.

Day Fifty-Eight

I didn't wake up a happy-chappy today. I awakened on the verge of becoming that insane, crazy person I'd spent the last few weeks trying incredibly hard not to be. My phone remained absent of response from *The Irishman* and naturally, my blood boiled and hands developed ideas of further text messages.

I could slap myself; put my hands on either side of my head, flip my legs up like a yoga goddess and really kick the shit out of my stupid face with my ridiculously flexible feet. What good would texting him again accomplish?

I'd lost my position of power and mystery, become needy by admission of attraction by urging him to take things beyond admiration of one another's underwear. What the hell was wrong with me? I thought I'd given up on the validation of male opinion?

The Irishman did eventually text back. He'd been intoxicated the night before, ploughed a golfing cart into an ATM, made off with fistfuls of cash and entered a high-speed police chase. The golf cart had since been impounded and the cash dispersed to the RSPCA since several birds were harmed in the making of the thirty kilometre dash. To say that I was annoyed he couldn't multitask and text back was an understatement.

I was too irritated to bother responding. I should never have sent him a message or given any inclination I wanted anything more—even if it was just sex! Needless to say I spent the rest of the day kicking my own ass for breaking my own rules. Even when he texted me again later, I didn't respond. I already decided the leprechaun would have to find a new pot of gold.

I chose the path of least resistance. Dating *The Irishman* would be fun on multiple levels, but I wasn't prepared to toss myself down the rabbit hole again, regress and make more mistakes. I was worth someone's time, energy and desires. So, I decided to keep moving forward, see multiple men and hope I'd eventually meet the one for me.

I planned to do a bunch of other stuff, too, like count the beans inside bean bags, hustle street urchins for food scraps and join Greenpeace, but I was a one step-at-a-time kind of girl and I only had two feet.

Day Fifty-Nine

I can't remember much of this day; not because I cleared out a liquor store, got wasted on shandies and skipped through a magical field of delectable mushrooms, but because it was more boring than re-runs of English crime-fighting drama.

I had *The Mother* to play with after work; that was something. We picked daisies from long grass, made necklaces while laughing like Mickey Mouse on crack as we skipped into the sunset. We really went shopping; spent money that neither of us had, but enjoyed the pleasure of one another's company over piping hot coffee and caramel slice. I also enjoyed the fact that my family and I were reconnecting again after years of sitting on the sidelines of each other's lives.

Whilst married, I'd isolated myself and relied only on my partner for compensation of emotional need. I'd since realised there were other people that loved and wanted to be part of my crazy little world, even if it was just to select toenail polish on a Thursday night.

The Mother—simply put—was brilliant at helping me amalgamate the broken pieces of my life since divorce. She helped calm my fears over finances, move into my new apartment and even soothed the savage beast after two major boyfriend break-ups. She dealt with my fluctuating moods and indulged—with much deep breathing and contained eye rolls—my colourful sex life with relative ease.

Tonight we walked, talked and perused merchandise with out-of-control price tags. We consumed coffee by the gallon—neither of us truly human without it—and worried about a future without self-service petrol stations or children's books without unicorns. Every night needed to be more like this, filled with love, laughter and just a touch of common sense.

Day Sixty

I love Fridays and Fridays love me, though not for any reason other than the blessed promise of freedom. I suspected Friday love was a truth for most people. Friday was the start of the weekend and brimming with potential to find and behold happiness. Whether I indulged in booze, boys, sport or ill-advised tattoos, the possibilities had always been and would be endless.

This particular night—on a whim—I agreed to meet a friend I hadn't seen for over twenty years. We'd gone to primary school together and had reconnected via social media, but never said more than a few passing words since coming-of-age.

Life was like that; easy to get caught up in the repetitious cycles of work and play. Whether that was the result of life narrowing or mere laziness in staying connected, I didn't know.

Okay. I lie. I was just decidedly lazy.

The Primary School Buddy had sent a few private messages over the last week. I'd brushed them off as quickly as I'd been brushing off *The Cockney*. I had no idea why I pushed people away, but it had become a bad habit I chose to break tonight.

I was curious regarding his desire to meet after all this time, but as our written conversations evolved, it was clear that he wanted a little more than I was willing to give. I needed to review my photographs on social media. Low cut tops, perfectly quaffed hair and a pouty smile were not exactly a recipe for innocent intent.

The Primary School Buddy implied a long-standing attraction, but

113

also urged that we rekindle our forgotten friendship. I was all for exiling him to the friend-zone; anything more was simply a thought too far. It begged the question: Could men and women be friends without ulterior motive? Could men and women only be friends if one or both were already in a relationship with someone else? Would the pull of the opposing gender ultimately be too strong for any friendship and the boundaries become blurred?

Too many 'what ifs'.

I spotted him outside the coffee shop we agreed to meet. One arm was draped casually over the back of his chair, presumably waiting for me as he chatted hurriedly into his phone. A business call? It ended as his eyes roamed the length of me with undeniable heat. I knew then that this was not the same boy I remembered from the schoolyard; he was all grown up and perving on my curvy bits.

We embraced warmly, kissed cheeks as the Europeans did (though I had no idea why) and then headed inside to order coffee. His was a flat white—an excellent choice.

I had theories about a man's coffee request and its significance. For instance, a flat white suggested contentment based on simplicity—hot milk and a shot of what everyone prayed to be good quality coffee. A latte was a little bit 'Mr Fancy-pants'. A tall black represented a highly strung individual with possible dairy intolerances. I could go on, but this was only the summation of a bored writer who generally dated flat whites or cappuccino lovers.

Anyway, we settled in for coffee and a lengthy chat. I listened to the ease in which *The Primary School Buddy* spoke about life, love and his flourishing career. He was particularly goal oriented and not afraid to try anything. He'd travelled the world and believed his truth that life was a journey meant for detailed exploration. I couldn't disagree on any particular point, just the part that involved suggestions regarding the two of us drinking more caffeinated beverages between his sheets before breakfast.

Cheeky bastard.

After a relatively comfortable hour of talking, we headed to a local bar that I knew to be *The Cockney's* watering hole. Why I remembered that particular titbit of information while on a date with another man, I'd never know. Yet, despite being aware that I was drinking with someone else and that *The Cockney* was away on business, I couldn't help but look around for him in the crowd of unfamiliar faces.

I sipped my house cider while *The Primary School Buddy* swigged down a Corona. He sought to make me laugh often with his enthusiastic storytelling and inappropriate wit. He was entirely too successful in this venture and I soon forgot about *The Cockney* and thoughts of sending him an impromptu message.

I was actually caught up in the reunion, moved by *The Primary School Buddy's* passion for life and thirst for knowledge. I thought that via intellectual stimulation attraction might grow, but I remained uncompelled to kiss him even though he often prompted the moment to occur!

After multiple attempts to generate an uninvited lip collision, I decided to head home. I allowed him some small measure of connection via our hands—not that I had a real choice in the matter. His vice-like grip was inescapable and I ducked and weaved the awkward goodbye moment by virtually running for my car.

Safely inside my car, I smiled, appreciative of the hot pursuit, but also glad to be alone. I was even more pleased that I didn't surrender to another's desire. Friendship was severely underrated!

It was now a firm belief of mine that men and women didn't always have to connect on a sexual level to seek gratification. Intellectual conversation teamed with an abundance of laughter and mutual admiration could be equally satisfying for different reasons. I just wished it was easier to seek it from those with a cheeky smile and an underlying agenda.

Day Sixty-One to Sixty-Five

*D*ays passed without much intrigue. I'd lived life, paid bills and made nice with friends and family. I thought often about messaging *The Cockney*, but since his social media posts indicated he was leading a busy life touring the streets of the big smoke, I didn't believe he really wanted to hear from me; I don't know why I thought this, just suspected it to be true.

I received word from *The Irishman*. He'd crossed my thoughts every so often, mostly because he was now the white whale in my collection of men. He was also untouchable—a memory from the past like so many others. Pursuing the unobtainable would label me cannon fodder and I was done with that avenue of self-harm. *The Irishman* was also hung up on a previous lover. I was gunning for my sexless leprechaun to be a shy guy, but it turned out (I'd since discovered) that his reluctance was based on an inability to move forward. He was shackled to his past as much as *The Ex-Squeeze*.

My pride was wounded and given the frequency of these occurrences, I needed to investigate whether my personal hygiene was up to scratch. Thankfully, since I hadn't explored every range of emotion with this man, I no longer cared how that story might have ended; time to move on once again.

He found love again with someone from his past and I decided to be happy for him. Not every moment in time could or should be a personal triumph. Sometimes there had to be an appreciation for the accomplishments of others and now that *The Bestie* had returned from her holiday, I saw no reason to continue wasting time on emotional back alleyways with paths to nowhere. So, despite yet another failed attempt at constructing a relationship with a man, I focused on the relationships that truly mattered— friendships.

Besides, there was no reason to wallow when my phone was inundated with messages from potential new lovers and there was a massive tub of peanut butter somewhere in the cupboard with my name on it. Paired with a bag of marshmallows and a nice hot coffee—happy days ...

Day Sixty-Six

Call me crazy, many have done so, but I joined a new dating site with a vast database of hot, single men. My phone vibrated incessantly with new messages and my mind had been blown by how popular my profile appeared.

The photo was modest and my intentions honest. I wanted to make friends, but also wanted everything in a man without sounding greedy and unrealistic. My expectations were perhaps far too high; attraction of the mind and body as well as someone to be a companion? I was more likely to be redirected to a site matching me with a labradoodle!

This morning I assessed myself in the mirror, trying to analyse what it was about me that screamed 'temporary'. My perky new breasts couldn't possibly be the problem—they'd defy gravity even after I'm six feet under. My skin was luxe and physique mostly in pique condition after all the hiking I did before work. I was fairly certain I was funny—not stand-up comedian quality—but enough to draw a smile from the harshest critic. I was also a nice person at the core which had to count for something.

While I continued to stare at the familiar reflection, it dawned on me that perhaps it wasn't any one particular thing that attracted varying forms of negativity, but a state of ever-changing circumstance—the call of fate if you will. Some things weren't meant to be, like fat-free peanut butter or ice-cream that never melted.

After this reflection, I sat snuggled up on my sofa, flipping through social media and answering messages from friends and family, content to just be, enjoy life and roll with the punches. When my phone unexpectedly pinged at me, a little thrill coursed through my veins. I'd been answering other messages for several minutes, but this was the sound of the familiar, one I automatically connected to *The Cockney*. The green light flashed and my finger trembled over the screen …

It wasn't him.

A new message had been received—a direct result of the new dating site. Curiosity evaded me. Perhaps it was a direct result of my mirror self-evaluation or perhaps I really missed my football-loving, pub-frequenting, green-thumbed cockney.

'Hi,' the message had read. Unoriginal, I ignored the text for several minutes, certain it would be another night-crawling, booby-grabbing, waste of my time. 'I don't think I'm tall, dark or handsome, but I'm average, white, and don't gag when I look in the mirror.'

I snickered, amused. He'd caught my attention so I figured that checking out his profile would be harmless. I was friend-shopping and he lived several thousand miles away, ate children for breakfast and considered sweat pants luxury day wear—he was immediately marked as 'temporary' by my brain.

I named him *The Iron Man*. Why? That was exactly what he was; a transient triathlete in town for a week to compete in one of Australia's most gruelling competitions. He also confessed to drinking peppermint tea and spending more time on a bike seat than was scrotally healthy, but I gave him a free pass on account of his comedic pick-up lines.

'I really like your profile,' he'd continued, 'and though I'm only here for a short time, I'd love to meet you for coffee if you're interested?'.

Intrigued, we chatted for several hours, bantered about inconsequential subject matter and then I eventually agreed to meet depending on our schedules. I had to verify that it wouldn't clash with my plans for world domination, but things looked open after dropping a bomb on whaling vessels in the Atlantic and stocking up the cupboard for the pending zombie apocalypse.

A massive part of me was annoyed that I was about to do it again, waste time on notching the bed post rather than slamming on the brakes and waiting for Mr Right. Then again, that day might never come and fun memories would be lost while I debated morality and today's interpretation of the modern woman.

Needing some solid, outside advice, I phoned *The Bestie* and argued my case with her. She found my spread-leg journey rather entertaining since I'd been married and faithful for the better part of my youth. Exploration was healthy and a definite must, or so she believed. So I relaxed my promiscuity alarm and allowed my life to run its course.

Day Sixty-Seven

*A*nother Friday night, another party; so many wanton images caressed the mind when the word 'party' was evoked. Alcohol, a plethora of bad choices and the certainty of a hangover automatically sprung to mind in association with this rather ambiguous word. Since the night was intended as a girl's night out, it also begged the question of whether we'd curtail to expectation or defy the odds.

Unfortunately, we defied expectation and rounded up like a bunch of geriatrics at a retirement home. 'Party' was a loose term designated to our little gathering. We had dinner—nice with sufficient conversation and excellent cuisine. However, half the table spent the night with their noses buried in their phones. Perhaps this exemplified my generation now; social niceties dispelled as we made room for the technological era to possess our lives and ability to communicate effectively.

On the other hand, social media ingeniously connected multiple personalities on a single forum for quick and relatively risk free interaction, but, its negative facets included the blind promotion of introverted behaviour and social awkwardness. A lot of people these days had no idea how to mingle. Take *The Bestie*, for example; with close friends and family she was often carefree and well spoken, but placed in a room full of people in which she was unfamiliar … she floundered.

Tonight was no exception. We were all acquainted, but most

123

girls slapped photos on social media and chatted intermittently about the very things they were advertising on their news feeds. Admittedly, I was just as bad, opting to text *The Ironman* versus listening to pointless banter. No one noticed which was sad, but the fact that I wasn't bothered by their inattention was perhaps more unsettling. When did I start to take the company of my friends for granted … again? When did I decide it was acceptable to whip my phone out during dinner conversation and ignore those present?

Yes we laughed and yes we had a lovely time mingling when the limelight had shone upon each of us, but by eleven, we were all just eager to get home. I stayed at *The Bestie's* house, too tired to make the drive home and possibly too intoxicated to attempt it. We chatted briefly about the night before she wandered off to bed with a headache. I stayed up later, talking to *The Ironman* and organising our date for the following night.

As I laid there between slightly chilled bedsheets, staring up at the ceiling, I contemplated the happiness to be found in this day. I started to realise that I needed to stop basing the success of this journey on a handful of moments boasting smiles, but rather, overall life satisfaction. There was no doubt that happiness could be achieved via the accomplishments of others and the ridiculous conversations between friends, but it was mostly acquired through my acceptance of the good, the bad and the ugly of day-to-day adventures.

How I viewed the world was entirely dependent on my level of ever-evolving maturity. I could either choose to be happy or choose to be sad. The greater question was whether I was also strong enough or brave enough to know the difference between choice and circumstance.

Day Sixty-Eight

*T*oday I woke up early to torture my body with a hike up the local gorge chased by a run back down; all together it was six and a half kilometres of sweaty goodness. I knew *The Bestie* wouldn't come with me so I didn't bother to ask. She was broken from the night before and still feeling ill; not a surprise given her headache and the family dramas circling her aching mind. So I soldiered on alone, but promised to go back with sustenance.

When I returned with frothy coffees, lollies, painkillers and breakfast, her little face lit up like a Christmas tree. It was a simple gesture to be kind to someone I cared for and yet, the rewards of such an act were vast.

Random acts of kindness were an absolute necessity to my continued growth!

With my good deed done for the day, I contemplated my forthcoming date with *The Ironman*. I was nervous—I shouldn't be. I didn't have any expectations or promises for tomorrow. Perhaps because our late night chats revealed his self-confidence eclipsed mine and his sexual desires were more—shall we say—kinkier than I was accustomed to, I faltered. His fetishes weren't dressing up like a dog and begging to be patted or even being flogged with a spiked baton while he yelled 'I've been a bad boy!'. I referred to posterior activities that had absolutely nothing to do with siting down to an innocent coffee!

Anal. They actually had a name for it. He might like being

jabbed up the bum with a giant dildo, but I figured if it were actually pleasurable, people would pay airport security to rough them up looking for non-existent drugs. Even if this sexual avenue of backdoor knocking was quite common these days, I'd decided he could go and rap his knuckles elsewhere.

I still had intentions of going through with the date. I was bored, searching for friendship and hoped the night would culminate with *regular* sexual gratification—without the poo particles on the bed sheets!

Towards late afternoon, I headed home to get ready and left *The Bestie* to her power-eating session. I wasn't sure if she'd make it up the stairs after gobbling down all the food I'd bought, but I figured she'd roll around on the floor until the bloating went down or yell for help when she needed to pee.

At precisely seven-thirty that night, I locked eyes on *The Ironman*; vivid images rolled across my mind; him shaking a big, black dildo over his head and singing, 'give it to me baby, aha aha'.

The Ironman was better than imagined; a little taller than me with short dark hair and gorgeous moss-green eyes. His smile was captivating and his lips simply inviting. Attraction was instantaneous and I groaned inwardly—my bed springs were getting a workout that night.

We immediately eased into comfortable conversation as we hopped in my car and headed for dinner. I thought it would be awkward, but *The Ironman* never seemed to run out of things to say, including an endless barrage of compliments which made me blush incessantly. He wasn't quite capable of making me laugh like *The Cockney*, but why was I thinking about him at that moment? A dreamy triathlete yanked me from the car, grappled my waist and pulled me closer for a completely unexpected kiss and I was thinking about my Brit!

That seriously happened after minutes of knowing each other. I was surprised by his quick advance, but when his malleable lips touched mine, I forgot all reason.

I melted into his embrace and let him drink from my lips like a man starving for the taste of my essence. Tongues met and breath intermingled. It was a dance in which I was intimately familiar, just unexpectedly exploring after ten minutes of meeting!

When we parted we were both breathless and a little dizzy—an after-effect we discussed over dinner and wine. *The Ironman* refused to take his eyes off me and never stopped telling me how beautiful I was. I'd never been so spoiled for compliments or regarded quite so highly. It was refreshing.

We headed back to my place after dinner. He received the extra-short tour of my apartment and found his way to my bedroom without invitation. He was brazen, removing his clothes and slipping between my cool, crisp sheets before I gave permission.

In hindsight, bringing him back to my sanctuary was no different than his expectations as he patted the mattress beside him, studying me with those eyes of promised pleasure.

And weird stuff …

We spent hours wrapped in each other's arms, me mostly pulling him north since he spent most of the time burying his face in my nether regions. I wondered if the man would ever need to come up for air, a piece of cake or perhaps a towel, but, like all my luck with men lately, his tongue skills were to compensate for other failings.

No, he wasn't plagued with a tiny penis or hairy Chewbacker testicles and no, he wasn't born with three nipples or a forked tongue. He definitely didn't disappoint me, just couldn't really satisfy me, either.

The man just wasn't able to get it up!

Too much time in the bike saddle meant there was no real happy ending without the help of some little blue pills and since he was in total denial of the situation, I had to overcome this hiccup by commandeering my battery operated boyfriend to finish the job. What a bust.

I was now certain that the next guy I'd meet would probably be a thirty-something-year-old mama's boy who liked wearing my high heels and ate my lipstick when he thought I wasn't looking.

Ugh.

Day Sixty-Nine

I barely slept a wink and it wasn't because *The Ironman* finally found wood; he snored like a freight train—so loud I was certain the neighbours would complain. Like all men, he tried to palm the nostril-noise off as having a bad case of the flu. Lies. The guy had serious sinus issues.

I dropped him back at his hotel a little after nine; both incredibly sleepy and famished after a night between the sheets. We also had things to do that didn't involve each other. I spent the day cleaning the apartment and attempting to watch a few DVD's and was constantly interrupted by *The Ironman* who continued to message me despite our clean break that morning. It was odd reading texts regarding my beauty, how much he loved my body, the way I talked about life and the world in general. It was unfathomable why he kept incommunicado after what I assumed to be a one-night-stand.

I was unmoved and reluctant to return the messages despite the flattery. Dropping him off at the hotel was like finishing a book, but for some reason, he was asking me to re-read the last few chapters—confusing. That was why when I received a text from *The Military Man* shortly after, I opted to read another book.

The Military Man wanted to drop by for a chat; code for us having a one hour deep and meaningful conversation followed by: let's get naked and satisfy each other. I immediately said 'yes' because he was my go-to for confusing guy situations and I was certain he'd explain *The Ironman's* pursuit.

If you just read this, I imagine first thoughts might have been … slut. I would not condemn you for it, but until you've walked a mile in another's shoes, no one should judge the path of another. I'd come from a relatively sexless marriage; a sweet and generous man he had been, but he'd also forgotten that I was both a woman and a wife with needs.

I made a promise to myself to never deny my thoughts, feelings or desires again and today that meant bedding men with rippling abdominals, killer thighs and moves that made me moan like a porn star. I still ultimately sourced relationships of substance, but since I'd been hurt more often than not lately, I saw no need to hurry into the arms of permanency.

So, when *The Military Man* came over and we had our deep and meaningful conversation followed by a ridiculously out-of-this-world bedroom romp, I didn't feel bad that *The Ironman* was the furthest person from my thoughts. What I did feel bad about; the flashing green light on my phone—a message gone once again unanswered to *The Cockney*.

Day Seventy

I woke up this morning feeling deliciously sore in all the right places and ready for more. Unfortunately *The Military Man* was predisposed, so despite better judgement, I agreed to meet with *The Ironman* again. I figured his flaccid behaviour had to have been a one off and strangely, I was curious about his motives—wanting to get to know me better.

So did someone else I knew ...

I read the latest message from *The Cockney*. He'd been having a dull time in the big smoke, lonely and bored without the company of good friends. He sent me a few pictures of the places he'd seen and asked what I'd been doing since we last communicated. I smiled fondly, genuinely engaged. Today I learned more about his family and the places he'd travelled. *The Ironman* was due to arrive on my doorstep, but I didn't want our back-and-forth to cease. I enjoyed the conversation without agenda and especially liked how he made me laugh.

A knock disrupted everything. It seemed as if neither of us wanted to pursue the present—me with my date or him with work. Reality was a jarring reminder of the moments we should grab a hold of more often, but neglected in lieu of circumstance or obligation.

'It was really great chatting with you, I was starting to think you'd lost interest,' he'd said.

'Definitely good to catch up,' I'd answered, 'I'm sorry I have to

131

bail on you.'

'Can't say no to a hot date ...'

Panic set in. How did he know?

I put the phone away and answered the front door, still shocked. Surely it wasn't possible for him to know my plans for the day, was it? Had I dipped my feet in paranoia and *The Cockney* was simply making a broad-termed joke? Yes, that had to be it. I was acting like an idiot while *The Ironman* stood there looking at me with grave concern.

'Hey, beautiful,' he'd said, 'you okay?'

I plastered a fake smile on my face, pushed thoughts of *The Cockney* aside and set about our day. We jumped in my car and headed north along winding beachfront roads and rainforest covered mountainsides. I listened to music, sung loudly and without embarrassment while pretending not to notice the possessive hand that covered my thigh.

The asphalt rounded the coast like a black ribbon loose in the wind against the horizon. The breeze caressed my hair and the salty taste of the ocean beyond touched my lips with the promise of a perfect day. We left the rain of town behind to pursue sunshine and frivolous activity, indulging in calorie laden food and exquisite caresses whether I was willing or not. I stopped bothering to object to his incessant need to touch me, kiss me or compliment me. In fact, it was entirely too pleasant and addictive to be that adored.

The damaged and still burdened part of my heart knew that sort of behaviour would eventually dissolve reluctance. Nevertheless, I immediately labelled *The Ironman* as unattainable, unlovable ... unrealistic. He was a one-night stand that wouldn't leave.

That night *The Ironman* stayed with me again. We were intimate on every level, my mouth bruised from the constant pressure of his eager lips. We explored, tasted, touched and laughed as lovers should. It was familiar and comfortable and never going to last. The dawn of the new day was a forthcoming reminder that the end would be here soon enough. I honestly welcomed it.

I'd become almost too good at letting go.

Day Seventy-One

*I*t would be fair to say that the monotony of the working day knew how to render the high of the weekend pointless. It didn't matter that my smile was genuine or that the slight skip in my step was because I was happy, I was at work and work pretty much sucked!

This happiness was not a derivative of an overly affectionate male. I was warm for the first time in a long time because I chose my own thoughts and feelings, decided what I needed and wanted in order to continue functioning on an emotional level. How easy would it be to release yet another floodgate upon my heart, allow pent up emotions to spill over the aorta and ventricles to seize common sense? How simple would it be to wrap myself up in pleasure and empty promises only to surrender to whimsy and intentions never fulfilled? I chose logic and sanity over crazy notions of non-substantial promises.

I chose me!

Anyway, given that it was the beginning of the week, it was also the day for new beginnings. I wasn't sure if that involved friendships, family, career or love and I suppose it didn't matter. All I knew was that things could no longer remain stationary, living moment-to-moment. I had to substantiate some sort of plan for the future, keep putting myself first, challenge myself and also try to achieve goals that would ultimately preserve my happy glow.

Unfortunately, the happy glow dissolved by lunch; the calendar reminding me that the electricity bill was due. Did I really need lights and hot water? The irrational part of me thought it'd be fun to use lanterns and start a fire in the living room, the rational part knew I was being a tool.

Day Seventy-Two

*T*he Ironman: strong, sexy, *transient*.
Why the hell did he persist texting and calling? I decided I had beer flavoured nipples—a delicacy indulged only by completely unattainable men. I couldn't hang onto someone I had genuine feelings for, but I'd been able to round up everyone else like a sheepdog on steroids. *The Ironman* was not everyone else, though. He'd sampled the buffet and tried a bit of everything on my menu. Surely he was full by now?

I pondered the thought for most of the day whilst pretending to work, chatting with colleagues and rubbing my poor, distended stomach. Why I decided to eat an entire can of beans for breakfast and why someone thousands of miles away would want to continue an impossible relationship was a mystery. Rationalising the thought was also impossible while my stomach pursued giving birth to demon spawn.

Need to know information—it was the worst case of gas I'd had in ages. I blamed it partly on the beans and partly on my dysfunctional body; all processing and evacuation procedures shut down in the presence of men. I would not fart, I would not poo. I was so clogged up I was a split second away from shoving an enema up my own ass. Four days—no poo. I was miserable, sore and wondering if it might not be beneficial to ask someone to ninja-kick me in the stomach so I'd explode like a New York City sewerage pipe.

Day Seventy-Three

'*W*hat a nice pair ...'
Intrigued, I looked at the abbreviated message on the home screen of my mobile and wondered if the seemingly innocent relationship *The Cockney* and I had steadily built just crumbled over some poor-taste booby joke. I wanted to open the message out of curiosity, but a part of me was reluctant, worried he'd mutated into all the other men and lost that special sheen I'd coated him in.

What if the attached image was a direct link to a porn site, an ex-girlfriend or a snapshot of a blonde jogger? Would I still be able to keep this man on the pedestal I'd placed him, knowing he might not be as special as I first hoped?

I bit the bullet and opened his message. The attachment was of a picture of a ripe, green pear sitting in the centre of what I presumed to be his kitchen bench. I giggled. *The Cockney* knew I was a wordsmith and cleverly concocted the message to not only touch base, but delight me with his humour—a success.

'Brilliant,' I'd written back, 'your "pair" has made my morning.'

'Glad to hear it,' he'd quickly responded.

I waited longer, phone in hand and hopeful he'd add to the conversation, but that was all. It was refreshing to look forward to someone's messages—namely his—since I regarded his quirky approach to our growing friendship highly. We'd still not set eyes on one another or scheduled a date of future meet and greet, but rather, taken pleasure in our unhurried and rather unorthodox approach to developing our union as friends.

I hadn't told my friends or family much about *The Cockney*. They were more interested in real-life entrants pursuing me than the quiet Englishman who texted randomly and without a relationship agenda. In fact, *The Bestie* thought it strange he hadn't taken up chase, but also advised that my current behaviour left little room in my life for someone of that calibre.

That was where social media became an issue; my life and those that came and went were often displayed with such vigour and disregard of appropriate activity that I often forgot who might be viewing my profile. I made no secret of advertising what I was doing or where I'd been and although I rarely mentioned a male counterpart, I suppose it could be implied.

Perhaps the reason *The Cockney* didn't pursue me with determined gusto was because he'd read between the lines. More often than not, I was taken by whatever flight of fancy blew in my direction and lately, the wind seemed to barrel into me with gale-force destruction. It was no wonder *The Cockney* loitered on the sidelines; he was trying to avoid getting swept up in a belligerent current with no end in sight.

Maybe it was time for me to start thinking about something other than the weather.

Day Seventy-Four

*F*riday; undeniably my favourite day and not because I had a momentous weekend planned. Today I was ecstatic because I spent time with one of my brothers and we'd decided—despite age differences and relative life-choice variations—to go on a holiday together.

He was early twenties and I'd most definitely met my thirties despite constant denial. He could be described as class and sophistication; I believed myself intellectual and casual. We were chalk and cheese—determined given the various situations that had affected us uniquely as individuals—to come together and celebrate our renewed vigour for life. We were thriving and pleasantly surprised that common ground could be accessible between siblings. So in the dappled afternoon sunlight we sat cross-legged on *The Parent's* sofa and organised the trip of a lifetime.

We were going to Borneo.

Random, right?

That was how I liked it—interesting. My life had been off-kilter for so long that it seemed fitting to choose a destination far removed from usual choice. Orang-utans and jungle paradises were exactly what the doctor ordered and we were both excited to mix luxury with adventure. We'd also be exploring deeper connections with one another and traveling off the beaten track to discover and enjoy what life might offer.

I was so pleased to make this decision—pleased to have

organised it with someone I love and respect. In fact, I was so pleased that I immediately posted the good news on social media. In a matter of minutes my status was flooded with notes of congratulations and 'likes'; it was also only minutes before a private message from *The Ex-squeeze* came through.

'Hey,' he'd written, 'I see you're going to Borneo.'

I couldn't have been more shocked to hear from him. It had been months since we'd last spoken and he'd left me with the very real impression that he cared little for my wellbeing. I was angry that he chose now to upset my good mood with such a trivial, stupid statement.

Of course I'm going to Borneo, you idiot, I just fucking posted it.

I didn't actually voice that opinion, but I was seriously tempted. My hesitation to reply must have prompted further exploration because he quickly began typing again.

Shit.

'I'm jealous,' he'd said. 'You're going to see some amazing things. I bet you could even smuggle a monkey back in your cleavage.'

He really had no right to be thinking about my cleavage, regardless of the potential to hold furry animals hostage between the voluminous pillows.

'Hey,' he'd continued, 'I've been thinking about you a lot lately. I just really wanted to see if you're okay. I hope you have fun in Borneo.'

I was two seconds from smashing my forehead through the front door. What did he care if I was okay? I was at such a loss for words that I ended up staring blankly at the screen, my fingers twitching in anger. After all this time he contacts me to tell me he was thinking of me and jealous about my upcoming holiday? Any emotion and affection I'd once felt was now summed up as valuable time wasted on entirely the wrong person.

I'm going on a holiday, I reminded myself. There really was no need to allow this minor interruption to stir a brand new cascade of feelings no longer welcome. I'd have a wicked time with my little brother and come home refreshed and positive about the future.

'Thanks,' I'd ended up typing back. 'I'll let you know if customs quarantine me.'

He replied with a smiley face picture that I really wanted to pin to the back end of a spiky pineapple and shove up his ass. That had

to be good 'getting over your Ex' therapy.
It didn't matter—I was going to Borneo!

Day Seventy-Five

I remember standing rigid behind my kitchen counter, forehead knitted together in concentration, a sticky knife balanced dexterously between my fingers. Ideally, I should have been looking down at my dead, creepy neighbour who'd informed me that he could access my apartment via our manholes, but unfortunately, I was immersed in the complex world of cake decoration.

Today was *The Baby Mama's* baby shower and I'd made it my mission to become Betty Crocker and bake a layered sponge from scratch whilst indulging other incredibly talented delights I should have paid a bakery to do.

I may have looked super-cute in my pink, woollen jumper, tousled hair and flour smudged cheeks, but I was gaining weight by the second. It had become an unfortunate situation of: one bit of icing for the cake, one bit for me. I couldn't keep my fingers clear of sweet debris and found myself eating left-over melted chocolate since I couldn't bare the sacrilege of sugary waste.

Breakfast consisted of: peanut butter stuffed Oreos coated in chocolate, fresh cream and berries, leftover sponge cake and marshmallows. There was also the extra lollies I somehow managed to shrug free from their packaging and inhale.

The Bestie was busy assembling her own creations, though she wasn't nearly as desperate to ride the sugar high with me. She nibbled delicately on the sweet treats but didn't overindulge to the point of activating her upchuck reflexes.

While I continued to irreversibly damage my teeth and intestinal tract, we worked on the party games and packaging the props to decorate on location. It was a shock that *The Bestie* and I were organised enough to bring the entire party together. I usually preferred a sideline activity and yet, here we both were in the thick of diaper hampers and baby wipes.

I had no idea that a newborn would need so much stuff. I imagined they would suckle like a calf when hungry, burp like a pig when well fed and sleep like a sloth the rest of the time. Apparently they also got bum rashes, cried incessantly and generally wiped out the rest of your adult existence with their ever-consuming emotional needs and financial burden.

Why did people have children?

By the time the baby shower kicked into full swing, *The Bestie* and I were exhausted; we'd cooked, decorated and greeted about thirty strangers all toting essentials for the newborn. We should have asked everyone to bring money. *The Baby Mama* was destined for destitution before the baby even cracked her uterus!

The fun and games also went down a treat as we sniffed unlabelled baby mush in a bid to guess their contents. We laughed at the tales of older mothers and cried just a little bit when one of the guests informed us she was a stripper, ripped off her dress and proceeded to show us how best to manoeuvre a stainless steel pole. We informed her that she'd attended the wrong party and sent her on her way. At least we'd saved *The Baby Mama's* grandmother from death-by-heart attack.

All-in-all, despite the cheap show and sterilisation procedures required on the decking balustrades, the elderly remained alive, the sugar highs continued late into the evening and everyone was pleased with attendance and frivolity. It was a lovely Saturday and I went home a happy, fat woman.

Day Seventy-Six

*T*oday I woke up afflicted with diabetes; body swollen and certain I'd die. I'd over-eaten the junk food from yesterday's party and subsequently was unable to leave my bed. I felt sick and sorry for my fat self and yet, completely uncompelled to stop. I was still dipping into the party favour bag and shovelling chocolate-coated liquorice into my mouth all before 10.00am!

I could say I eventually emerged, went for a really long run to burn energy and excess calories, had a shower and then turned vegan, but that would be a lie. I stayed in bed, flicked through channels and continued to eat the left-over lollies until my tongue became black and my head spun. I also decided to worry about the repercussions in the morning.

Day Seventy-Seven

*A*lthough the working week once again came around and with it, the downward turn of lip and sombre mood, I wasn't entirely taken with manic Monday mayhem. I'd had a rather simplistic weekend enjoyed mostly solitary that had been drama free—a particularly nice way to start the week.

Now back at work, I slogged through paperwork, gave *The Boss* a bit of a hard time over a possible pay rise, accepted stern rejection and then carried on until clock-off time. Nothing thrilled me more than knowing the day would end with a late night adventure—an evening involving dinner and theatre.

A local production of The Wizard of Oz—assembled by a talented group of high school seniors—was due to be performed eloquently and riddled with humour. Work colleagues insisted upon my attendance to watch their eldest daughter perform in greasy green makeup while bantering with broomsticks and munchkins. It was a fantastic show that I thoroughly enjoyed despite the incessant singing.

I'd never been one for the theatre; it stemmed back to my adolescence when I'd dated a particularly attractive young man with a severe penchant for Madonna and musicals. I should have realised then that my dreams of kissing his cherry pink lips were dashed as his unfolding homosexuality blossomed during our three month tryst. He dragged me to every theatre production, musical film and chorus-line imaginable and yet, I never once thought it strange that he had better hair than me and insisted on only wearing Calvin Klein.

Last I heard, he lived in the city with his boyfriend and they'd adopted a baby.

A real one ...

From this country.

Anyway, after the theatre, we all went out to dinner. We dined on pasta, salad, salmon and far more garlic bread than could possibly be healthy. Since I'd sugar-loaded on the weekend, I avoided sweets completely. *The Bestie* licked her dessert plate clean, effectively doing the kitchen-hand staff out of a job.

The table next to us laughed at her antics—in particular—a cute blonde guy with dreamy blue eyes who smiled at me more times than I could count. It was nice to be noticed, even if it was *The Bestie's* plate cleaning technique that drew the attention.

We all parted ways around ten o'clock, sated and happy; a nice way to end a Monday and a perfect way to head into the rest of the week. I may have had Show Tunes circling my mind as I fell asleep and thought about my gay Ex while I contemplated downing a heart burn tablet, but at least it was trivial, comfortable and no real cause for any complaint.

Day Seventy-Eight

*T*oday I clock-watched. I couldn't help it. There were very few clients to consider and I'd been so efficient the day before that there was even less for me to do today. I wandered aimlessly around the office, collating papers and shuffling them from desk-to-desk, appearing productive.

I doubted whether *The Boss* bought my tactics. She watched me from the corner of her eyes, never offering to assign me special projects; unless the list included: rosters, archiving old cases and re-organisation of client files. Naturally I rejected such suggestions as they sounded like hard, boring work.

At lunch time I crab-walked past the café to avoid looking at all the goodies and made plans with *The Bestie* to exercise that afternoon. I was still exercising solo in the mornings, but figured since Saturday's binge, I owed it to my talking thighs to work off the extra cellulite chatter.

As the sun set on yet another day, we walked in companionable silence. We often did that—*The Bestie* and I lost to our own thoughts. I was trying to calculate how many shoes it would take to fill my closet and the dollar value attached and I assumed she was thinking about the previous night's dessert.

As it turned out, she'd been thinking about her upcoming birthday. I reminded her that she was still in her twenties and that the old lady beside her was due for a wheelchair. She politely reminded me that I was only mid-thirties, not middle age and if I continued to carry on, she'd pop my breast implants and really give me something to complain about.

Day Seventy-Nine

I was full steam ahead with *The Bestie's* birthday plans; not something I usually indulge because organising events generally left me with a bitter taste in my mouth. Case-in-point: my wedding. We had grandiose ideas of a 1930's style reception; a lavish dinner in a ballroom of a luxury hotel, intimate wedding in a garden and as little expenditure on flowers and non-consequential items as possible. It evolved into a massive fare with miniature rose posies, expensive champagne and a dress that became a compromise due to rising expenses.

I'd backed out of the deal with months to spare, grabbed the now Ex-husband by the hand and dragged his confused ass to Thailand to elope. Hardly the romantic ideal, but I hadn't been able to see past the enormity of my growing credit card bill. I also hadn't appreciated everyone's over-inflated opinion of how *my* wedding should be.

As it turned out, I should have run to another state, started a new life and given the whole idea of marriage a miss. I should not have married the man I loved because he was my best friend. I needed to marry a man that I was passionately *in-love* with, who made my knees tremble, my heart beat uncontrollably and also made it impossible for me to imagine any part of the rest of my life without them.

That would be true love or at the very least, my perception of it. Hence, I'd lost enthusiasm for planning events. I was now shite at following through and let down often by those invested in the project. I even remember being twelve, organising a movie date with mates and being stood up. Later in life, work Christmas parties turned into dysfunctional arrangements where everyone was in different places at different times.

This was not a reflection of my coordination skills; the mishaps were a direct result of all the idiots I tried to collaborate with. This was why I chose to have one final stab at planning something enticing for *The Bestie's* birthday. She deserved my commitment to the project if for no other reason than she was my very closest friend.

It helped that I'd limited the party-goers to two—me and her. It was easier to ensure timing and scheduled activities occurred in the proper sequence and without the distraction of others less inspired; plus, I'd decided to pay for everything and since becoming a single lady, I was now a cheap prick who had no intention of forking out for anyone else.

So far the plans were coming together quite nicely. I had breakfast sorted and a day at the beach followed by some pretty exciting nightly festivities. I was looking forward to it, even if it was still several days away!

Day Eighty

oday was the day to hear from everyone I hadn't talked to in a while. *The Ironman* was first. He professed his undying love and revealed plans for our future nuptials. Completely opposed to the idea, but not against the free plane ticket he'd mailed, I was floored by the gesture. He truly believed that a relationship between us could work. I was more realistic; we lived in completely different worlds. The easy companionship between us was irrelevant when I wasn't even sold on our validity.

Maybe I owed it to myself to see him again and explore what we had a little further. With a free plane ticket in the post, that was exactly what *The Ironman* expected I'd do, but I'd never curtail to the idea of marriage. Hell no, probably not ever.

The Primary School Buddy was the secondary message; he wanted to catch up for a little adventure sports. I was curious, though it wasn't unusual for men to promise me a good time; promises often led to me paying for dinner, them vomiting all over the front seat of my car—or worse still—almost getting back-doored because correct insertion during intercourse confused them!

<Insert scepticism here>

Anyway, *The Primary School Buddy* and I last interacted over coffee and a few drinks. He painted me as this incredibly smart and beautiful woman that would be better invested in a relationship with a likeminded individual. I agreed on all accounts and asked him to point out that potential match when he came along. I don't think he found my joke amusing.

Romance was removed from the table despite his constructed arguments. I had no interest in someone I used to punch in the balls as a kid. As adults, chemistry was absent, but I was curious about what sort of adventure sports he had in mind.

'What's up?' I'd messaged him.

He responded almost immediately with, 'I was thinking about white water rafting tomorrow. Do you think you can wrangle a day off work?'

I really didn't have to think about that too hard.

Hell yes.

I promptly messaged *The Boss* and asked for some personal time. Since I very rarely went on holidays or fell sick, she was quick to respond positively; she may have also been tired of my paper shuffling and wanted someone serving the public with a vested interest in getting work done.

'I'm in,' I'd written back to *The Primary School Buddy*.

I remember beaming, not because I was given the day off work, but because I'd be doing something I never thought I'd do. White water rafting had always been one of those activities I hoped to be brave enough to one day pursue and now I planned the possibility of imminent death!

'Great. I'll pick you up just before lunch.'

Sorted.

The third message was from *The Military Man*. He was feeling particularly lonely and wanted a cuddle—also known as—let me bury my face in your boobs. I never hesitated to accept his company; we had no expectations to exist as anything other than friends with benefits. Despite our amazing sexual chemistry, he was actually a great guy to talk to. Neither of us had any idea what we were doing half the time, but it was fun figuring everything out together.

As the night rolled into shifting in the warm embrace of a good friend and ideal lover (the kind that goes home), I went to sleep with a smile on my face, knowing that the next day would be fun-filled, action-packed and the perfect lead up to a weekend spent lavishing *The Bestie* with much deserved attention on her birthday.

Day Eighty-One

What a day I had to look forward to and what a way to pump adrenaline through the veins! I couldn't be more excited about the prospect of tumultuous water and dangerously sharp rocks on the horizon. I was about to be deposited into a situation outside my comfort zone. I wasn't scared—not much—I was apprehensive placing myself in obvious danger. *The Primary School Buddy* kept me entertained with his ever-insightful conversation and desire to impress—a positive distraction in many ways.

I drifted in and out of focus as I listened to his financial chatter and thought about the last few months-to-date. I'd been on so many adventures both emotionally and physically, it seemed almost fitting to continue this journey by exploring new avenues of excitement that didn't culminate in either gender's opinion.

As we arrived, conversation drew to a close. I sprung free from the car and immediately queued outside the transport bus with thirty other passengers, all united in common interest. I beamed. We weren't waiting for ice-cream or a one way ticket to Mauritius, but the joyous rush of an adrenaline fuelled day led by what I hoped to be an accomplished tour guide.

A gentle tap on the shoulder roused me from my excited daze. 'Hey, don't I know you?'

I blinked, turned side on and assessed the tall blonde man with dreamy blue eyes smiling down at me. He indeed looked familiar, but my brain was operating on a completely different tangent. I was thinking about rubber dinghies and frothing, cold river water.

'Yeah, yeah, I remember now,' he'd continued, barely waiting for my reply, 'I saw you the other night in that pasta restaurant with your friends.'

What were the odds of ever running into him again, especially now as we boarded the same bus to succumb to a watery grave?

'Oh, hey, yeah, I remember you, too.'

'You going white water rafting?'

I pointed to the bus with a puzzled expression. Did he think I just liked to ride these things with random tourists for fun?

He shook his head, perhaps realising what a goose he'd sounded like. 'Sorry.' He then held out his hand. 'My name's *The Engineer.*'

I shook the newly outstretched hand. 'Nice to meet you, this is my friend *The Primary School Buddy.*' I shoved him in front of me, offering him up for inspection. He frowned profusely as *The Engineer* eyed up the competition. Men were so interesting sometimes.

The Primary School Buddy quickly dragged me onto the bus and distracted me with tales of his latest overseas travel. I never noticed *The Engineer* take the seat behind us or watch me the entire journey like a crazy, psychotic stalker (all of which he disclosed to me at a later date).

Anyway, the bus didn't take long to wind along the river's road or the tour guides to shuffle us off and into the waiting dinghies. We were briefed on safety and given vests, helmets and instructions on how to prevent death and dismemberment. My favourite was a reminder to hang on; as if that wasn't bloody obvious!

We were off before I realised, the tumultuous river throwing us in multiple directions and splashing us with burning desires to escort us to its watery depths. I squealed often—not with fear— with delight. I was thrown left and right, evicted from my seat and saturated from head to toe, but I loved every minute of it.

The entire river journey took roughly two hours and I was water-logged and soggier in the toes than expected. My ears were partially blocked and I was certain there was a fish lodged in my left nostril. I couldn't thank my friend enough for suggesting such a manic experience. I had no doubt I would do it again if someone else was willing to pay for it.

As the day drew to a close and *The Primary School Buddy* and I headed towards his car, *The Engineer* came running up to me. 'Did you have fun?' he'd asked, somewhat breathless.

'I had a brilliant time!' Never a truer statement was spoken.

He started to nod as if he fully expected me to respond as such. 'Hey, I know you don't really know me, but I was wondering if I could get your name and maybe your phone number?'

The Primary School Buddy looked less than impressed, but was gentlemanly enough to realise he had no control over the situation or my actions, so he just silently fumed.

I gave *The Engineer* my name, but held back from the phone number; blondes weren't my type. I truly appreciated the forward notion of asking for exactly what he desired, but I wasn't sure. To follow this road yet again—especially with *The Ex-Squeeze's* recent message still floating around inside my head—it misaligned with my desires.

'I promise I'm not a freak, I was just hoping I could take you out for dinner sometime soon.'

I felt like a bit of a shit making dinner plans in front of someone that also vied for my attention. *The Primary School Buddy* knew my position, but it was still awkward to choose another in his stead. He didn't wait to hear how the conversation ended and hopped into his car and started the engine—my cue to get in, too.

I snatched the pen *The Engineer* had poised between dexterous fingers, hastily scrawled my digits on his forearm, then jumped into the car beside my friend and endured his scowl all the way home. I'd like to say that I spent the whole ride trying to make it up to him, patting his bruised ego and promising another adventure-filled date sometime soon, but I didn't. I sat in silence, thinking about the day and how much fun I'd had, how much I'd laughed and how much I didn't care whether or not a boy *may* like me. I was content to relish the great time I'd had with my friend—even if he continued sulking over an incident I had very little control.

'You're going to go on a date with him, aren't you?' *The Primary School Buddy* had asked, breaking the silence.

I shrugged. I really hadn't thought on it and I really didn't care. In that moment I was just happy being me and living life.

Happy Friday …

Day Eighty-Two

Not entirely unexpected, but *The Primary School Buddy* tried to gnaw my face off with his presumptuous lips last night. Can you believe it? We went back to his place after white water rafting, had a few drinks and had talked and laughed like we'd done during our last catch up. We reminisced about the day and how funny it was to watch me get smashed by errant river waves. Everything had gone smoothly; he'd gotten over *The Engineer* and we were actually having a good time—until he tried to kiss me.

No exaggeration when I say I drowned in saliva. Not only was the kiss absolutely horrid, he held the back of my head so I couldn't escape! I struggled for precious air while his lips swallowed my mouth and chin, drool escaping in puddles by my feet. I wasn't able to evacuate the building fast enough after that.

He accepted my dash to the opposite end of his couch with dignity; he didn't push for more and didn't frown when I used my t-shirt to wipe down my face. I suspected he'd seen this kind of reaction before since he passed me a tissue box.

He drove me straight home where I then stood under a hot shower for as long as humanly possible. *The Primary School Buddy* wasn't unattractive—we had zero chemistry, kissing me only served to make the whole situation feel *wrong*.

Thankfully, today a new day and *The Bestie's* birthday celebrations were occupying my mind. I had amazing adventures planned to coincide with the local street festival as well as the overindulgence of food and alcohol.

We started the day with breakfast—nothing too grand but there was no way I was cooking so I took her to a little café that had rustled up eggs benedict and drinkable coffee. We laughed and chatted and of course, she was incredibly grateful for the gesture.

With bellies rotund and hearts happy, we moved onto the beach; our favourite nudie spot to grab a good dose of sunshine on the pasty white bits. *The Bestie* avoided shitting in the ocean again and I narrowly avoided sunstroke with my overzealous desire to brown my breasts. There were no streakers (old men with saggy balls) or errant children straying from the watchful eyes of their parents.

It was a perfect day without incident. We were happy, warm and content with the activities-to-date. Everything else that might have happened from that point forward was merely a bonus. Breakfast and sand surfing may sound boring to some, but to us it was bliss.

Once we soaked up enough UV rays to negate the point of sunblock, we headed home for a few leisurely drinks before getting ready for our night in the city. My wallet was at the ready and despite a dwindling bank account, irrelevance crept in as we sipped our sugary wine.

Hours later we stood roadside, *The Bestie* and I grinning from ear-to-ear as we watched the annual street parade pass in a flurry of vibrant colour and joyous music. Floats of unimaginable variety were decorated with people of all ages, gender and race. They'd come together to celebrate the region in which we all resided.

Children squealed with delight, zipping in and out of bystanders while we laughed at their antics, excited for what was to come. Night quickly approached and with the passing floats, streamers and dancing paraders, our stomachs rumbled. We lingered not on the bustling streets, but headed to a restaurant poised above the crowd and overlooking the water.

We ordered cocktails and entrees and indulged in a sumptuous arrangement of delicious Greek food. As more food was distributed, the parade ended and we waited with baited breath for the fireworks to begin. As they crackled over the horizon, *The Bestie* and I smiled fondly at one another.

'Thank you,' she'd said, 'This has been the best birthday ever.'

Of course it was.

I grinned, rather pleased with myself.

As the fireworks drew to a close and diners packed up and left, I gazed over my shoulder at a particularly rowdy table in the corner of the restaurant. There were at least ten or twelve of them, bottles of wine sprawled across the table top and plenty of empty dinner dishes; they'd had plenty of fun that night, their ongoing levity only served to make my grin widen.

I wondered if they were all family or just friends, coming together to celebrate the festival or a special occasion like me and *The Bestie*. I supposed it didn't matter either way. It was simply joyous to see contentment on every face that smiled in my direction.